Cast For Death

ALSO BY MARGARET YORKE

THE OXFORD DON MYSTERIES

Book 1: Dead in the Morning

Book 2: Silent Witness

Book 3: Grave Matters

Book 4: Mortal Remains

Book 5: Cast For Death

CAST FOR *Death*

MARGARET YORKE

JOFFE BOOKS

Revised edition 2026
Joffe Books, London
www.joffebooks.com

First published by Hutchinson Publishing Group
in Great Britain in 1976

This paperback edition was first published
in Great Britain in 2026

Cover art by Dee Dee Book Covers

ISBN: 978-1-80573-409-3

PART 1

I

The body lay just beneath the surface of the river, the hair streaming in the tide, legs splayed with the movement of the water, arms spread, the face downwards. Above, unaware of what floated so obscenely close to them, people surged along the terraces outside the concert halls, and theatregoers crossed to the parking lots beside the Festival Hall, their voices and the sound of car engines noisy in the air.

Against the clear night sky, London's great buildings stood out, etched in brilliant detail. Dr Patrick Grant, Fellow of St Mark's College, Oxford, leaned against the parapet overlooking the Thames and approved of what he saw. The river flowed darkly past, a jet mirror studded with the silver reflections of the lights on each bank; he stared across the water, and turned over in his mind the problem of where to eat. The evening had not gone as planned; he had intended to spend it with Liz Morris, whom he had known since his own undergraduate days, but when he reached the Fantasy Theatre where they were to have seen *Macbeth* together, he found not Liz, but a message to say she could not come. No reason was given. It was too late to find another companion, so he had turned in the second ticket; it had been sold to a large man in a corduroy jacket who had flowed across the seat-arm between them and had eaten toffees throughout the performance.

And Sam Irwin had been out of the play. It was to see him, as well as the much-lauded Macbeth of Joss Ruxton, that Patrick had come up to London. He had enjoyed the play, whenever his restless neighbour stopped fidgeting, for the verse was well spoken and the director had allowed the words and the action to exert their own power over the audience without extravagant distractions of his own. But a programme note said that Sam Irwin was indisposed, and Macduff was played by someone unknown. The play was at the end of its run in a season which was to conclude with *Henry VIII*, so there would be no other chance to see Sam in the part.

Patrick had planned to invite the actor, whom he and Liz had first met in Austria four years before, to eat with them afterwards; now, it seemed pointless to go alone to an expensive restaurant, though he must have some sort of meal before returning to Oxford.

At this point in his reflections he saw it: something white in the river not far away. Patrick's attention concentrated on the spot where the object had broken the surface of the water a short distance upstream. There it was again, and now he identified it: it was a hand, white and ghostly, the fingers gently curled as the water parted over it and left it exposed. He stared in horror: this was no mystic, legendary arm offering a sword: this was grim death.

Someone else saw it in the same instant: a woman, who gave a shriek. There were more shouts and cries. Footsteps pounded on the pavement, and people came to lean over the parapet beside Patrick, staring at the sight. In a very few minutes the police arrived and were soon down on the bank under the wall, hauling the body ashore. It was a man dressed in dark clothes against which his hands and his face showed white as he lay sprawled in the light from above. His hair, sodden and therefore darkened, looked like mahogany in the lamplight.

Shocked murmurs broke out among the gathering crowd. Their fascinated absorption in the tragedy filled Patrick with disgust; nothing could be done for the drowned man himself and officialdom had taken charge, so he slipped away. He had seen enough of sudden death and there was nothing to hold him here.

His appetite had gone, though, and he drove straight back to Oxford without dinner.

II

Liz telephoned at half-past nine the next morning. She had waited until then, to see if Patrick would call her first. Surely he must wonder what had prevented her from meeting him at the theatre?

'Ah, Liz,' he said, answering promptly.

At least he recognized her voice, she thought wryly.

'What happened?' he went on, sounding unconcerned.

'I was abducted by two hi-jackers,' she said.

'No, Liz, really. What held you up?'

'Mrs Pearce in the flat below fell and broke her hip. I had to see her into hospital,' she said. Why bother to tell him about all that had to be done — the daughter in Dorset informed, the suitcase packed, the milk stopped. He wouldn't be interested. It had taken hours, for the daughter was out and had to be tracked down by way of neighbours. 'It happened too late for me to get in touch with you before you left Oxford,' she added. 'You got my message?'

'Yes, thanks. I'm sorry you couldn't make it.'

'So am I,' she said. 'Did you enjoy it? How was Sam?'

'The man who had your seat unwrapped toffees throughout,' said Patrick. 'And Sam wasn't playing. It was some stand-in.'

'Oh, why? Is he ill?'

'Indisposed, it said in the programme. That could mean anything from appendicitis to a hangover, I suppose.'

'Poor Sam. And how disappointing not to see him,' said Liz. 'He does seem to be unlucky.'

Sam Irwin's hoped-for come-back in the theatre had not amounted to a great deal, though he had worked steadily since Patrick and Liz had met him. There had been a season at Stratford-upon-Avon in small roles, and he had appeared on television at intervals, but he had not found fame.

'Yes,' Patrick agreed. 'Well, anyway, I'm glad you're all right.'

'Did you really think I might not be?'

'No. You'd have said you were ill, in your message, if you were.'

'You might not have been given that part of it,' Liz said tartly.

'You sound annoyed,' said Patrick, surprised.

'Oh no, I'm not,' said Liz. 'Why should I be?'

Why indeed? Their relationship had never gone beyond the affectionate friendliness of their undergraduate days. Patrick regarded her as someone he could pick up and cast aside at his own whim; he always enjoyed her company but sought it rarely. She accepted this and was not really surprised when fresh confirmation of his limitations, as now, appeared. In a sense it was a restful situation; Patrick was a safe, undemanding figure from the past and an amiable companion for the present: no more.

'I thought you sounded a bit off,' he said. 'I was going to ring you,' he added, 'to see what had happened. But I thought it couldn't be much.'

Not much: she recalled the night before; poor shocked Mrs Pearce in pain; the trek to the hospital; the telephoning. It had seemed quite a lot at the time.

'We'll try again,' said Patrick. 'Something else, since *Macbeth*'s finished.'

'Yes. All right. That would be nice.'

Would he suggest a definite date? She waited, but he didn't. Perhaps he was going away for the vacation. She asked him.

'Oh, here and there for a few days, perhaps,' he said. 'Not abroad.'

'I thought you might be off to Athens for Easter, since you've got so bitten with Greece,' said Liz. Patrick had visited Greece several times in recent years and had become so enamoured of the country that he now found it difficult to plan visits elsewhere.

'No. But Dmitris Manolakis is coming over here,' said Patrick. 'That policeman, you remember, who was so efficient in Crete.'

'Those vases. Yes.'

'And those deaths,' said Patrick.

'You had a hand in sorting it out, too, didn't you?' Liz said mildly.

'A minor one.' And literally, for his hand still bore a small scar.

'Is he coming on holiday?'

'Yes. He's got some relations over here whom he wants to see, and Colin's going to show him round at Scotland Yard. Then I'll take him about a bit.'

'Is his sister coming too?' Liz had heard about her, after Patrick had stayed with Manolakis in Crete.

'She's married now,' said Patrick.

'Oh, good.'

Patrick thought it a pity.

They ended their conversation with no plans for meeting.

III

Oxford in the vacation was a pleasant place. There were far fewer cycles about, and even fewer undergraduates. The tourist season was only beginning; small groups appeared in college quadrangles, but the hordes of summer had not yet arrived. The trees were in bud, leaves swelling with the promise of spring, and the forsythia hung great yellow sheets in the gardens of North Oxford. On Headington Hill the blossom was out. Patrick spent the weekend after his trip to London reading a book of literary analysis by a colleague, and writing a waspish review of it. On Tuesday he set off to meet Manolakis at Heathrow. He was glad of this diversion. Most of his colleagues had dispersed to various places — the married ones to their homes, the unmarried to friends or abroad — and St Mark's was quiet. He was usually glad of some weeks clear to devote to research, but a book he had been working on was complete ahead of schedule, and he had time to spare. Manolakis's letter announcing his visit had been a surprise; he was coming, he had written in his flowing foreign hand, mainly for pleasure; he hoped there would be time to meet. Patrick read more into this than was apparent; once before Manolakis had combined business with pleasure and had solved a crime; this time he could be on the trail of another. He replied at once with an invitation to stay at St Mark's and said he would meet Manolakis when he arrived.

With the new stretch of motorway open, the journey to London by road was now easier than ever. Patrick sped along in his dark red MGB. He still enjoyed its novelty. After his Rover was stolen and then found smashed beyond repair, he had spent weeks wondering what to replace it with, and had tried out numerous rather sedate saloons before choosing a sports car. There was no need, since he was unmarried, to consider the problem of space. So far, only his sister Jane had had the temerity to tease him about his revised image.

Manolakis's plane was due at eleven-forty. Patrick planned to take him in to London straight away, for a general look round before making plans for the rest of his stay. He knew that the Greek had been in direct contact with Detective Inspector Colin Smithers; Patrick hoped to be present when Colin showed his Greek colleague some of the secrets of the Yard, and altogether he looked forward to his friend's visit. Manolakis doubtless had in mind specific places he wished to see, and Patrick would happily conduct him to others which should not be missed.

The miles slid by, the car purring along through the spectacular cut above Aston Rowant. Patrick took the turnoff for Marlow to join the M4, and drove down the linking escarpment which by-passed the riverside town behind a blue Mercedes. He followed it round the roundabout outside Marlow and up the road which climbed through the woods to the junction with the Henley road, where he turned left to pick up the motorway. There was a lot of traffic here, going in both directions, and he was forced to crawl behind a van which the Mercedes had managed to pass. As they went in procession past a church and the turning to Maidenhead a black flash, a dog or a cat, suddenly sprang from the side of the road between Patrick's car and the van in front. There was nothing he could do to avoid it, for if he braked the car behind, already much too close, would crash into him, and he could not swerve away because of the oncoming traffic. He stamped for an instant on the brake but had to release it at once. There was a considerable thud, and Patrick slowed down, pulling in to the side of the road as he did so. The cars behind reformed and sorted themselves out as he got out and walked back along the road to see what he had hit.

The dog, for that was what it was, had been flung on to the verge by the force of the collision and now lay motionless on the grass. It was a black poodle, and it was dead. The law obliged you to report the death of a dog to the police, and your own morality to tell the owner, but this one wore no collar. Well, the owner could not be far away, having doubtless been exercising his pet on the nearby common. Or her pet. Men, Patrick thought, did not own poodles.

He laid the dog closer to the hedge, out of range of other motorists, drove on to the roundabout and circled it to turn, then took the road across the common. But there was no sign of anyone whistling or calling; no one seemed to be searching for the poodle. By the time Patrick had found a police station, described what had happened and left his own name and address, half an hour had passed.

He hurried on towards Heathrow, the bright day dimmed a little by the incident, time short now if he were not to be late for Manolakis.

The plane had already landed but the passengers were not yet through customs. Manolakis, in a light brown suit and bright blue tie, was among the first through the doorway. He beamed as he greeted Patrick with many warm remarks and much hand-shaking. The flight had been perfect: no bumps; he had seen both Venice and Mont Blanc. He had never been out of Greece before.

'Haven't you a coat?' Patrick asked, as they went to the car. A sharp wind blew round the airport buildings.

'I have one for the rain in my baggages,' said Manolakis.

'You'll need to wear it for the warmth,' said Patrick.

'Your city is very fine from the sky,' said Manolakis. 'I have seen Windsor Castle and the Thames river.'

'We're so near, I thought you might like to see a bit more of London now, before we go to Oxford,' said Patrick.

'That would please me very much,' said Manolakis. 'I would like to see the Tower of London, please.'

'The Tower!' Patrick had anticipated a sentimental trip to the Elgin marbles in the British Museum, but had not foreseen this. 'I've never been there myself,' he confessed. 'Right. The Tower it shall be. You'll see quite a bit of London on the way.' Then he had an idea. 'We'll go by boat,' he said. That would make a fine introduction to the splendours of the capital.

The Greek was clearly impressed as they drove through Hyde Park, past Buckingham Palace and down Whitehall; Patrick explained everything as they went along.

They left the MGB in a car park, and Patrick urged Manolakis to put his raincoat on, for it would be breezy on the river. Before embarking, they found a pub which looked suitably atmospheric, and over their beer and ham sandwiches Patrick enquired about Manolakis's wife and three children; all had sent him affectionate messages, and so had his sister. Then they went down to Waterloo Bridge to catch the boat.

The voyage was a good idea. Sunlight filtering through the wispy clouds emphasized the varying hues of all the buildings as they passed. Patrick pointed out the most notable, and when they approached the Tower he launched fluently into a description of the young Elizabeth in the rain, a tale equal to any Greek legend. Patrick himself was quite moved as they passed within the huge walls wherein so much tragedy had dwelt. There were groups of schoolchildren on holiday walking around, and a number of tourists, but so early in the year it was not crowded and they could move about freely. Manolakis was impressed by the vast suits of armour for horse and man; it was all rather different from the Archaeological Museum in Heraklion.

'We go back by river?' he asked eagerly.

So they did. Patrick pointed out a police river patrol boat as it went by.

'Last time I was in London I saw a dead man taken out of the river,' he said.

Manolakis made clicking sounds with his tongue.

'Who was it?' he asked.

'I don't know. Some suicide. He had red hair,' said Patrick. Until this moment he had almost forgotten the incident.

'You did not ask the name?'

'No. There was nothing I could do. It was no concern of mine,' said Patrick.

'It is not like you. Not wanting to know why,' said Manolakis.

'Plenty of people jump into the river,' said Patrick. 'You can't wonder about them all.'

'We do not have many suicides in Greece,' said Manolakis.

While they talked he was gazing about him.

'So big,' he said. 'So very big. And beautiful.'

Patrick felt proud. Manolakis was right: London was, indeed, a beautiful city.

'We'll go to the Houses of Parliament another day,' he said. 'And Westminster Abbey.' He felt a sudden lightening of spirit; the slight depression brought on that morning by the accident with the dog had gone.

'"Latest swindle case,"' read Manolakis as they passed a newspaper seller. 'What is swindle?' His English was so good that Patrick was surprised by the question. He explained. 'Ah yes. I write him down when we get to the car,' said the Greek.

'Do you still carry that notebook around with you?'

'Oh yes. He is very useful,' said Manolakis. He had a habit of noting down new colloquialisms whenever he met them and then producing them, used perfectly in context, soon afterwards.

'I will buy the paper. I will read him later. It will be good for my English,' said Manolakis. 'It is so strange to hear it all about us.'

In fact they had not heard it all about them, in Patrick's opinion, for so many people in London spoke in other tongues.

'I'll buy it,' he said.

'No, please!' Manolakis put up a hand. 'You know me, Patrick. You understand my speaking. I must practise with other people.'

He was right. And there was the unfamiliar money too.

'I got me some small money on the plane,' said Manolakis, and he stepped forward to carry out his little transaction.

On the way back to Oxford, they stopped in Marlow for dinner. The visitor was swift in admiration of the river scene. Swans obligingly swam past, and the weir lent drama. It was very un-Greek. By the time they got to St Mark's and Manolakis had been installed in his room, fatigue after his journey and the subsequent tourism hit him, and he went to bed forgetting his newspaper. Patrick sat down for a few minutes alone, gathering himself after the day. He was tired too; he had overlooked the fact that being a good host is often exhausting, no matter how welcome the guest. Idly, he turned the pages of the *Evening Standard*. With Parliament in recess there was a dearth of political news and plenty of space for domestic items. Several valuable old paintings had been stolen from a house near Leamington Spa while the owner, a Birmingham businessman, was out at the theatre. A party of Americans, including a senator, had arrived in England for a varied programme of talks about matters concerning pollution of the atmosphere; there were pictures of Senator Dawson, of Princess Anne preparing for the Badminton Horse Trials and another of Ivan Tamaroff, the Russian pianist who had defected to the west eight years before and whose son, Sasha, a celebrated violinist, was soon to make his first visit to London where the two would perform together. At the foot of a column on an inside page a small paragraph caught his eye. *Actor's death*, he read, and below the heading:

> *The inquest on Sam Irwin, 44, the actor whose body was found in the Thames last Friday night, has been adjourned. Mr Irwin was currently appearing in the part of Macduff in the production of Macbeth at the Fantasy Theatre.*

Shock made Patrick's mind a blank at first. Then, as he unfroze, horror succeeded. Sam had been dead, not ill, that night: dead, and in the river.

But it couldn't have been Sam whose body he had seen. That man had red hair, and Sam was dark.

PART 2

I

Next morning, at breakfast, Patrick showed Manolakis the piece in the paper.

'He was your friend? Oh, what sadness,' said Manolakis, about to tackle the bacon and eggs which Robert, Patrick's scout, had produced.

'But why? How?' Patrick demanded, brandishing the paper in the air above his coffee cup.

'Suicide. You say there are many in your river.'

'It must have been.' But why had the inquest been adjourned?

'You will be finding out, I think,' said Manolakis.

'Yes.' It was dreadful news; he must learn what had happened, and when the funeral would be held. The coroner had probably given permission for this at the preliminary hearing; as far as Patrick knew, Sam had no close relatives; he had always seemed very much a loner. Liz must be told, too.

While Patrick telephoned her, Manolakis gazed from the window at the Fellows' garden. It was so green outside, and the daffodils under an ancient cedar were like pictures of England in springtime which Manolakis had seen. An elderly man in a shapeless jacket was walking over the velvety lawn, smoking a pipe. A gardener, Manolakis supposed, not realizing that he was looking upon the Master of St Mark's.

Liz, just arrived at her office, was very surprised at the identity of her caller, and shocked by what he told her.

'Oh, how terrible! Do you mean it was Sam that you saw that night?'

'No, it couldn't have been. That man had red hair — bright red, it must have been, as it looked distinctly auburn even when wet.'

'He could have dyed it, for Macduff,' said Liz. 'You might not have recognized him, from a distance.'

It was true that Patrick had not looked closely at the body; he had not wanted to become involved. Now, the thought that the dead man might, after all, have been someone he knew and from whom he had walked away, filled him with remorse. He would have to find out.

'You could be right,' he said.

'Please tell me, Patrick, when you know,' said Liz.

He did not have to explain to her the compulsion he would now be under; she knew.

'All right. I'll be in touch.'

He would, as this involved someone else and was not just a matter of friendly communication; though shocked by his news, Liz was detached enough to see the irony in the situation.

Patrick immediately rang up Detective Inspector Colin Smithers at Scotland Yard, and learned that it was indeed Sam whose body had been found near the Festival Hall. No one else had been fished from the river that night.

'Why didn't you tell me it was Sam?' fumed Patrick.

Colin had not known that Patrick was there when the body was found.

'I didn't know myself till just now — it's not a Yard case, the local boys are handling it,' he replied. 'But as it happens, a colleague had mentioned it to me — that's why I could answer you.'

'Oh, sorry.' Patrick knew he had been unreasonable. 'But what happened? Why has the inquest been adjourned?'

'They frequently are — to enable fuller enquiries to be made,' said Colin. 'Now, what about your Greek friend?' He switched the subject.

'He's here. You'd better talk to him,' said Patrick, and gave the telephone to Manolakis. He and Colin had never met, but both had been concerned with a case involving thefts from ancient tombs some time before. Now there was an exchange of polite platitudes on the line before the two policemen made their plans to meet. It was decided that Manolakis would go up to London the next day, spend most of it at the Yard, and then go on to visit some relations, returning to Oxford in a few days' time.

When all this had been arranged Patrick took Manolakis round the college; this was a lengthy business for there was a lot to see. Manolakis was not as impressed as American visitors by the antiquity of the building, for by Greek standards it was young, but he conceded that it was beautiful, and exclaimed in admiration of the library, where some old volumes could still be seen chained to ancient reading desks. In the afternoon they toured the city, taking in the Sheldonian, the Bodleian, and the Epstein at New College, then walked to the river where Patrick explained about Eights Week, Torpids, and the Boat Race, at which Manolakis marvelled. He had arrived just too late to witness this annual event, Patrick, a rowing Blue, lamented.

'You took part in this challenge?' asked the Greek. 'Wonderful. I admire you.'

Patrick was reminded of the Argonauts: Greeks today were still doughty seamen, but perhaps not notable oarsmen any longer.

'It was a long time ago,' he said.

II

Next morning they left for London. They had spent the evening at the Playhouse watching a revival of *The Importance of Being Earnest*, and Manolakis had been able to follow most of the dialogue, though Patrick had had to explain the nuances of the play. The theatre, with its panelled walls and rose-rust seating, had an intimate atmosphere which Patrick always enjoyed, and Manolakis said he admired it, though he thought the city, when they walked back to St Mark's after dining near the theatre, very quiet.

There was enough bustle in London to satisfy anyone, Patrick reflected, hunting for a parking meter near the Yard.

Colin said airily, when they entered his office, 'I won't invite you to join us, Patrick. I'm sure you've things to do and you've been here before.'

Patrick was chagrined; he had expected an interesting day. Perhaps Manolakis, being a policeman, was to see more of what went on within the Yard than even such privileged visitors as himself. There was also the possibility that the Greek had some official reason for meeting the CID.

'That's all right,' he said grudgingly. 'But tell me, first, what you know about Sam Irwin's death.'

'I knew you'd ask,' said Colin. 'There's not much. He lived in a bed-sitter in Hammersmith, and when he didn't turn up for the evening performance last Friday the rest of the cast thought he was ill, but he sent no message. However, it seems he sometimes got attacks of nerves, though he'd never actually missed a show on that account — not lately, anyway. Actors are expected to be temperamental.'

Manolakis had been listening to this with intense concentration, and now he asked for the meaning of 'temperamental'. The word was explained, and then Colin continued.

'No one at the theatre was alarmed at first. By the time they did start worrying, he'd turned up, in the river.'

'Any note?' Patrick asked. 'Any reason for suicide?'

'No.' Colin hesitated.

'He did not drown,' said Manolakis, pouncing.

'Right,' said Colin, and looked at Manolakis with respect.

'What, then?' demanded Patrick. 'Some sort of fit? A heart attack?'

'Yes. Just that,' said Colin.

'But how did he get in the river? You mean he died somewhere else and the body was thrown in? Good God, why?'

'Why indeed,' said Colin grimly. 'And why were there marks on his wrists and ankles as if he'd been bound, and fragments of sacking under his fingernails?'

'You mean he was tied up and chucked in? But he wasn't tied up when he was found.'

'No. Nor were there any weights to hold him down. Perhaps he couldn't swim. But he didn't drown.'

'Oh, my God,' said Patrick, now truly shocked. 'What on earth can have happened?'

'Routine enquiries are proceeding,' said Colin.

'But it must have been murder!'

Colin shrugged.

'Who would want to do it? Who on earth would want to kill poor, harmless Sam!' Patrick exclaimed.

'I don't know,' said Colin.

'He had an attack — he died, perhaps, from fear, when he is finding himself suddenly in the water?' Manolakis suggested, and Colin nodded.

'It's possible. If whoever threw him in knew he couldn't swim.'

'How was he identified?' Patrick asked. 'Were there papers on him?'

'No — a bystander recognized him. Odd, wasn't it? You didn't, but someone else who'd seen him acting did.'

Patrick might have done, if he had looked more closely.

'He'd dyed his hair,' he said.

'Yes. This woman — she'd been at some function or other in the Festival Hall, it seems — had seen him on the stage only a few nights before. He'd made her cry, she said, and she knew him at once. Remarkable.' Colin, not a theatregoer, found this hard to comprehend.

But Patrick understood at once.

'Ah yes. "What, all my pretty chickens and their dam at one fell swoop,"' he quoted. 'It's a very moving scene, that one — or should be. When Macduff pulls his cap upon his brows.'

'I do not understand, please,' said Manolakis simply.

'And nor do I,' said Colin.

Patrick explained how Macduff learns that his wife and children have all been murdered.

'Ah, I learn much from you, my friend,' beamed Manolakis.

'And I do, too,' said Colin. 'We're just a pair of simple coppers, Patrick, don't forget.'

'You must have heard the line before — it's such a tongue-twister — so easy to say "at one foul sweep",' said Patrick.

'Methinks I do remember,' said Colin, and Patrick was forced to smile. 'I'll let you know more, if I can.'

'I might have a look around a bit,' said Patrick.

'Well — there'd be no harm done,' Colin said. 'It could be quite a tricky one. You might hit on some point not obvious to us. Though we often get there in the end.'

'I know you do.'

'Patrick's hunches are often worth investigating,' Colin said to Manolakis, and wondered if the Greek understood the expression. He seemed to, for he nodded. 'Then we have to find the evidence to back them,' Colin added.

'I'll get along, then,' Patrick said. 'You've things to do, you two.'

And so had he, now.

PART 3

I

Sam's bed-sitter was above a dairy not far from Hammersmith Broadway. Patrick had expected to find it locked, but a police sergeant was there, being harangued by a middle-aged blonde in a tight red sweater and mock lizard boots.

'It's not as if there'll be rent coming in,' she said. 'I've my living to think of.'

'I'm sorry, Mrs Hulbert. I can't let you take it over yet,' said the sergeant. 'You won't be the loser, though, I'm sure. He owed nothing, you said.'

'No. Paid to the end of the month,' the woman grudgingly admitted.

'Well, then. It's not mid-month yet. You'll have plenty of time,' said the policeman.

Muttering about the need to clean up before finding a new tenant, the woman went away, casting a suspicious glance at Patrick as he stood on the landing.

'She thinks I'm another copper,' he remarked, entering the room. 'My name's Grant. I knew Sam Irwin.'

'Oh yes, sir.' The policeman, who was sorting through a pile of papers, looked at him sharply. 'Can you be of any help to us?'

'I fear not. I hadn't seen him for some time,' said Patrick. 'And I've only just heard about this.'

He looked round the room. It was large, with two long windows overlooking the street. There were a great many books in a case running along one wall, and an expensive high-fidelity record player, with speakers at either side of the room.

'He was quite a reader,' said the sergeant.

'He'd been a schoolmaster,' Patrick remembered. 'History — that was his subject. Yes.' It was confirmed as he studied the titles on the shelves; H. A. L. Fisher was well represented. There were also a number of books about musicians: biographies of composers and performers, and the librettos of some operas. Patrick took out *Falstaff* and looked at it curiously.

'Was he, sir? Where did he teach?' asked the sergeant.

'I'm afraid I don't know,' said Patrick.

'Let's sit down, sir, shall we?' The sergeant pulled up a chair and took out his notebook. 'Maybe you can fill in a few gaps for us, concerning the deceased.'

'What? Oh — very well.' Patrick, who had briefly forgotten why he was here because he had been so surprised to find himself reading what seemed to be *The Merry Wives of Windsor* couched in romantic Italian, put the book hastily back and sat down on the sofa, a loose-cushioned, comfortable one, but shabby. 'Had he lived here long?' he asked the sergeant.

'Two years. Didn't you know?'

'No. The last time I saw him was in Oxford about a year ago — he was on tour with a play. I never knew his home address,' said Patrick.

'Your full name and address, sir, please,' said the sergeant, becoming formal and Patrick supplied it.

'St Mark's College, Oxford? Then it was you who helped Detective Inspector Smithers with that Greek art job,' said the sergeant.

'You could put it that way,' agreed Patrick wryly. 'But how do you know about it? You're not from Scotland Yard, are you?'

'No, sir. I have my contacts,' said the other impressively. 'Bruce, my name is, sir. I suppose it was through Detective Inspector Smithers that you knew where to come today, as you didn't know the home address of the deceased.'

'Quite right,' said Patrick, who was still taking in the details of Sam's room.

'Not very luxurious, is it, sir?' remarked the sergeant. 'But these actors — up one minute and down the next. I'd never heard of him — not by name, that is — but I'd seen him on telly. That pays well, I think.'

'I imagine so. But unless you're in a series, it's not very steady,' said Patrick. 'He wasn't well known — he just never quite made it. But he was a very good actor.'

'Fond of music.' The sergeant waved a hand at the equipment and pointed to a long row of records.

'He was a cultivated man,' said Patrick. It was dreadful to be talking about Sam in the past tense like this.

'We're having a problem finding out about friends,' said Sergeant Bruce.

'Can't they help you at the theatre?'

'Not really. No one saw him much away from there — he used to vanish after performances, it seems. But no one had any harsh words to say about him.'

'I'm not surprised. He was far from harsh himself — he wouldn't provoke a harsh reaction in others,' said Patrick. 'He was a quiet, self-contained man, not at all like one's notion of an actor, performing both on and off the stage. What was he going to do when the season ended at the Fantasy? It has only a short time to run, I think.'

'Oh — has it? I didn't know about that,' said Bruce, making a note. 'The superintendent may, of course.'

So a superintendent was paying attention to this case: well, that was routine, no doubt.

'What do you think happened?' Patrick asked. He had better keep quiet about what he already knew, since perhaps Colin should not have told him.

‘Looks like suicide, on the face of things,’ said Bruce.

‘You’re taking a lot of trouble, then.’

‘There are some puzzling features,’ said Bruce. ‘Do you know if the deceased could swim?’

‘I’ve not the faintest idea, but I’d imagine so. Can’t most people, after a fashion?’

‘Not at all. You’d be surprised how many can’t,’ said Bruce. ‘Particularly older people. Most kids get a chance to learn these days.’

‘Hm.’ How old was an older person?

‘Perhaps you’d tell me how you met the deceased?’ prompted Bruce.

‘Oh, it was in Austria, about four years ago,’ said Patrick. ‘In a little place called Greutz. The village got cut off by avalanches from the rest of the world. We both happened to be staying there at the time.’

‘Ah yes. Not much you can do, cut off like that, is there?’ said Bruce.

‘Not a lot, no,’ agreed Patrick. But the experience had been far from uneventful. Sam, at the time, had shown unexpected resource by playing the piano for dancing when a power failure had put the discothèque out of action. ‘Why should he commit suicide?’ he asked now. ‘Were there bills all over the place? He seems to have been well ahead with the rent.’

‘No. There’s no sign of any serious debts,’ said the sergeant. ‘But this isn’t much of a place.’

‘Is there just this one room?’

‘Yes. He shared a bathroom on the landing below with two other tenants. No proper cooking facilities either — only that ring in the grate.’ The sergeant indicated a gas ring on the hearth. Then he got up and opened a cupboard. ‘He kept his stores here.’

Patrick saw sugar, a jar of instant coffee, a tin of soup, a packet of Earl Grey tea and one or two oddments. It was not unlike his own small store at St Mark’s.

'I expect he ate out most of the time. He wouldn't want to cook after the performance,' he said. 'And then he was away on tour quite often. Keeping a better place might have been uneconomical.'

'Maybe he toured to get away from it.'

'He toured because he took what work was offered, you'll find,' said Patrick. 'It's all clean and well kept.'

The walls were painted grey, and the curtains were a faded jade colour; an elephant-coloured haircord covered the floor, with a worn rug on it in front of the fireplace. The décor seemed more likely to be Sam's choice than that of his gaudy landlady.

'It's drab,' said the sergeant. 'Not artistic.'

'You're disappointed because he was an actor and didn't live in a Habitat setting, Sergeant Bruce,' said Patrick. 'It's anonymous, certainly, but Sam was like that; he was quiet, fading into the background. He took colour from the parts he played and then came to life.' Was that the only time? Had Sam lived only vicariously through his acting? 'Have you found any photographs?' Patrick asked.

'No, not one. There's no sign of a girl friend — or a boy friend, come to that,' said Bruce.

'If there is anyone they'll show up soon, won't they?' Patrick suggested. 'Weeping, and what-not?'

'I would expect so. If you think of anyone — or of anything else that might be helpful — will you get in touch with me at the station?' said Bruce. 'I'll give you the number to ring.'

'Of course I will, sergeant.'

Sergeant Bruce opened a drawer in a small cabinet and took from it a bottle of capsules, blue bullets, instantly recognizable.

'You know what these are, don't you, sir?'

'Indeed yes. Sodium amytal.'

'Right. If I'd these, and wanted to commit suicide, I'd take the lot, not jump in the river. Wouldn't you?'

'Er — yes. Yes, I suppose I would.' The question was a difficult one for Patrick to answer; though he often found life disappointing, he had never seriously thought of denying its challenge. 'Perhaps he didn't intend to commit suicide,' he said.

'Exactly, sir.'

Patrick had better not mention the marks on Sam's wrists, or the fibres under his nails.

'An accident, you mean?' he said.

'A gesture — a cry for help,' said Sergeant Bruce reflectively.

If he thought that, then he was ignoring the marks and the fibres too.

'Not just before a performance,' said Patrick. 'He was too professional. I know what you mean — I've seen it in Oxford, more than once. But Irwin would have waited until the play's run ended.' And he would not succumb to an attack of nerves at the end of a run, surely: the start, when he was perhaps unsure of his own ability, would be a more likely time. Besides, he would never have contrived the binding of his own wrists and ankles in a bid for help and sympathy. No, he'd snap completely, or not at all. 'Well, I'll let you get on,' Patrick added. 'I'm sure you'll soon get to the bottom of it, sergeant. We'll meet again, I hope.'

'I hope so, sir, I'm sure,' said Bruce.

'Oh — and give my regards to Inspector Smithers, if you're in contact with him again,' Patrick said blithely. Let Colin sweat, wondering what he had revealed of his privileged knowledge. Sergeant Bruce had been very forthcoming, on account, no doubt, of the fact that he had heard of Patrick before. But why did Colin know so much about the case himself when it was not a Yard matter?

II

Because he was already so close to the M4 motorway, Patrick left London by that route instead of joining the M40, up which he and Manolakis had come that morning. As he drove towards the turning for Marlow he remembered the poodle. By now, the owner might have been traced; it would be civil to stop, find out, and call to apologize for causing the death of the dog. Accordingly, he turned off the main road and went to the police station where he had reported the incident.

The constable who had been on duty then was behind the desk, and remembered the event.

'We've discovered the owner, sir,' he told Patrick. 'A Mrs Tina Willoughby. She lived on the common near where the accident happened.'

'Lived? Has she gone away? Did she move and abandon the dog?'

'Not exactly, sir. She's dead.'

'Dead? She died recently, you mean?'

'She was found yesterday, dead in bed,' said the policeman. 'We think the dog had been roaming wild.'

'Oh dear,' said Patrick. 'How sad. Was she an old lady?'

'No, sir. Not much above forty,' said the policeman. 'She'd been dead some time when she was found,' he volunteered. 'The dog must have got shut out of the house when she was taken ill.'

'She lived alone?' She must have, if she had lain dead for several days before being found.

'Yes, sir,' said the policeman, who was young and sometimes too enthusiastic to be wholly discreet. 'The inquest's tomorrow,' he added.

'What did you say her address was?' Patrick asked.

'I don't think I mentioned it, sir,' said the policeman. 'But the house was called Strangeways.'

'I see,' said Patrick. 'Well, I hope the death of the dog had nothing to do with her death. People get very attached to their pets.'

'I think you can set your mind at rest about that, sir. She died first.'

He seemed certain. Patrick thanked him again and left. Simple curiosity made him seek out the house, Strangeways, and a few minutes later he stopped the MGB outside it, a long, low, white-painted house at the end of a cul-de-sac on the edge of the common. There was no sign of anyone about, but he got out of the car, walked up to the door, and rang the bell. Some relative might be there, clearing things up, and Patrick still felt he owed someone an apology about the dog.

There was no response, so he turned away and was just lowering himself back into the car when a short woman in her mid-forties, with jet black hair, wearing white trousers and a black suede fringed waistcoat, appeared from the house next door.

'There's no one in,' she said.

'So I see,' said Patrick.

'You're not a relative, are you? Of Tina's I mean.'

'No, I'm not,' said Patrick.

'I thought not — just a friend. Well, you're in for a shock, then. Won't you come in for a minute, and I'll tell you about it?'

She was clearly bursting to talk; Patrick wondered if she made a habit of inviting unknown males into the house. He entered warily, lest she pounce on him.

But all she did was to sink down on an elegant, high-backed chair and indicate that he should sit on a brocade-covered settee facing her.

'Tina is dead,' said the woman. 'Suicide. She took sleeping pills — a whole bottle, I believe. She was found yesterday — she'd been dead several days. And her dog's disappeared. Funny how animals know, isn't it.'

'Disappeared?' said Patrick, bowled over by this torrent of speech.

'Quite vanished. She had a poodle — a black one. Quite a nice little beast. It was nowhere to be found when they took her away.'

This theory of suicide explained the policeman's reticence.

'Why would she want to commit suicide?' Patrick asked.

'I can't imagine. She seemed to have enough money — men friends, for ever changing. Everything she could want.'

'Lonely, perhaps? But you say she had friends—?' Patrick let the question trail off.

'She was divorced. Well — you knew that, didn't you? She still had her looks. Men came here from time to time.' She looked at Patrick consideringly as she said this. He was a man, and he was here. 'Of course you knew she was moving — she's sold Strangeways, and she was due to move soon — next week, I think.'

'I — er — oh yes,' said Patrick, studying the deep carpet on which his feet rested.

'I can't think why she wanted to leave here. But she's crazy about the theatre — must have got an actor boy friend, I suppose.'

'The theatre?'

'She's moving to Stratford-on-Avon. Or was, I should say. You knew, surely? Or hadn't she told you?'

'Well — er — no — she hadn't, as a matter of fact.' Patrick had got himself thoroughly enmeshed now. He hurried on. 'Did she leave a note? Who found her?'

'The milkman. Found Tuesday's bottle still on the doorstep. No, there wasn't a note. At least, I didn't see one.'

So this interested neighbour had been in the house hot on the heels of the milkman. How had they entered? Patrick waited, and sure enough his curiosity was soon satisfied.

'I knew where she kept a key, you see, outside. In the shed. She'd locked herself out once or twice by mistake. She hadn't put up the chain on the door — we got in easily. It was rather surprising, that. She usually bolted it, too.'

'And she'd taken sleeping pills?'

'Yes. There she lay — quite tidy — just the newspaper thrown down on the floor beside her.'

'The newspaper?'

'The *Telegraph*, it was. I noticed particularly. She always took it.'

Patrick's glance, when he entered the room, had taken in two papers, neatly folded, on a coffee table. He focused on them now: *The Times* and the *Daily Mail*; his and hers, he supposed.

'For which day?'

'Monday, of course. It was on Monday night that she did it. I suppose she read the paper in bed while she waited for the pills to work. It seems funny, though. I don't think I'd want to read the paper at a time like that.'

It did seem funny. What would one do under such circumstances? Read poetry or the Bible? Or listen to the radio? Patrick could not imagine himself in such a situation.

PART 4

I

Jane Conway recognized the sound of her brother's car as it turned in at the gate and drew up in front of the house. She had not seen Patrick for some weeks, so she went out to meet him as he unfolded himself out of the MGB.

'Well, what a surprise,' she said. 'Have you had lunch?'

What with one thing and another, Patrick had forgotten about it. At this reminder, he realized that he was hungry. He said so.

'There's bread and cheese, and the remains of some ham,' said Jane. 'Come and tell me your news.'

Patrick followed her into the house. She had been ironing in the kitchen, and he found a pleasant domestic scene there, with his nephew Andrew, now aged six, colouring in a drawing book at the table, and Miranda, almost two, playing with some wooden bricks. The children welcomed him with flattering joy. Andrew then resumed his task, but Miranda stood staring at Patrick with unblinking concentration.

'She remembers me,' he said, with fatuous delight.

'Of course she does, idiot. She's seen you a good few times before, though not lately, it's true,' said Jane. 'Sit down and talk to her while I find you something to eat.'

Patrick sat down at the table, facing Andrew, and Miranda at once stood leaning against his knee, still staring. Her unwavering gaze was solemn.

'What does a child of this age want to discuss?' he wondered aloud, staring back at her. She was fascinated, though he did not realize it, by her own twin reflections in his spectacles.

'Show her this book,' said Andrew helpfully, as one man to another, pushing one across to him. Patrick opened it at a page illustrated with ducks marching in line past some cows, but Miranda shut it firmly. Patrick approved her judgement. Holding her breath, she began to scramble on to his knee and reached out to seize his glasses.

'Hey, Miranda, don't do that,' he protested.

'Looking windows,' said Miranda.

'Yes, they are, but they won't be if you bash them,' said Patrick, pleased at this evidence of a possible philologist in the family. 'Jane, have you got Monday's *Telegraph?* You do take it, don't you?'

'Yes, we do — we may have it still. I'll look,' said Jane. 'Why do you want it?' She put the loaf, butter, cheese, ham and some tomatoes in front of him. 'Help yourself,' she instructed, removing Miranda and setting her back in front of her bricks.

'To see if it reports a particular news item,' said Patrick.

'Keep an eye on this mob, then. The papers are in the shed. An old boy in the village has started collecting them for re-pulping. It'll be there unless I've used it to wrap up rubbish,' said Jane. She unplugged the iron and put it on top of a cupboard above her head, where Miranda could not reach it, and departed into the garden.

Patrick cut a slice of bread and spread it with butter. It was warm in the kitchen; there was a pile of freshly ironed garments on the dresser beside a vase of cherry blossom, and a smell of baking hung in the air.

'Watch her!' warned Andrew, as Miranda set off across the room. 'She grabs things.'

On Patrick's last visit, his niece had been imprisoned in a play-pen when Jane was busy; now she seemed perilously free to roam at will.

'What's happened to her cage?' he asked.

'She grew out of it,' Andrew said. 'She screamed if she was put in it. You have to watch her all the time.'

It was true. Patrick snatched her back just as she caught hold of the ironing-board which would have collapsed on top of her, and held her securely until Jane returned with the newspaper.

'This child's not safe, left loose,' he said.

'Andrew's a good watchdog,' said Jane.

'But you can't let her out of your sight for a minute,' said Patrick.

'You can when she's asleep,' Jane said.

'You must get exhausted,' said Patrick, for the first time dimly comprehending the demands made by a young family.

'Oh, she plays for hours,' Jane said. 'She's very good. Here, Miranda, let Patrick eat his lunch. You go back to your bricks.'

Reluctantly, muttering to herself on a crooning note, Miranda obeyed, and Jane handed Patrick the paper.

'Here it is. This is Monday's,' she said.

'Ah, good. Bless you. I thought this would be the easiest way to get hold of it,' said Patrick artlessly.

'So that's why you graced us with this visit. I had wondered,' said Jane, lifting down the iron and plugging it in once more. 'What's this newsworthy item that isn't in *The Times*, then?'

'I'll show you, if I can find it,' said Patrick, and looked at the columns on the front page while he continued to eat. 'I should think it will be somewhere inside.'

There was silence for some minutes while he glanced through the pages, pausing to read the reports on the Midlands art robbery; a photograph showed the owner lamenting his loss and police investigations were continuing.

'Ah, here we are,' Patrick said at last. 'There, Jane. Didn't you notice it?' And he pointed to a few lines at the foot of the centre page.

Jane came over to read it.

A body found in the Thames on Friday night has been identified as being that of the actor Sam Irwin. Mr Irwin, 44, was currently appearing in Macbeth at the Fantasy Theatre, ran the item.

'Oh! But that's your friend! The man you met in Greutz!' she exclaimed.

'What is it? Can I see?' demanded Andrew, coming round the table to have a look.

'It's nothing you'd be interested in,' said Patrick hastily.

'A friend of Patrick's has had an accident,' Jane told him.

'Oh! Is he dead?'

Andrew's bluntness disconcerted Patrick.

'Er — yes, he is,' he replied.

'Car?'

'No. He fell in the river.'

'I can swim,' said Andrew. 'A bit, that is,' he qualified.

'I'm glad to hear it,' said Patrick.

'Out, now. Into the garden with you both,' said Jane briskly.

'Let me just finish this bit,' said Andrew, carefully filling in the ear of a tiger in the book before him.

'Come on, Miranda, let's get your boots on,' said Jane. 'You can go out and rake the grass for Daddy.'

Patrick watched while the children were bundled into anoraks and rubber boots and turned out into the garden. Jane closed the gate to the road.

'It's comparatively safe now,' she said. 'Andrew is very sensible. He keeps an eye on her. Luckily she loves dragging that toy rake up and down. I'll make some coffee. Have you had enough to eat?'

'Yes, thanks,' said Patrick.

'What is all this about Sam Irwin?' Jane asked. 'I never noticed that piece in the paper. But it might not have meant anything to me, even if I had. They don't say much about him, do they?'

'Perhaps there will be more after the final inquest,' Patrick said. 'But Sam wasn't very well-known. I was there when he was fished out of the river, although I didn't realize at the time who it was.'

'Oh, Patrick, no! Not again! Not another mystery death!'

'I don't know. But I'm curious,' Patrick said. He told her what had happened, and about the owner of the poodle.

'The *Telegraph* for Monday was beside her. That's why I wanted to read it,' he said.

'You think there's some connection?'

'I don't know. It could have been something else in the paper that upset her. Another death, one in the ordinary columns. Or it could have been just chance that the paper was there in her room,' said Patrick. 'But no one seems to know what really happened to Sam, so I'm going to find out if he knew this woman, if I can. She was interested in the theatre, the neighbour said. Neither of them left notes, which is odd. People tend to, when they intentionally kill themselves. It's a coincidence that needs to be investigated.'

'Why don't you just ask the police?'

'I don't want to make a fuss without cause. This woman's death is bad enough without stirring things up unnecessarily. She was going to move, any day now. It seems a funny time to commit suicide.'

'It does, rather,' said Jane. 'Maybe she couldn't face the thought of moving.'

'It was her own choice, Mrs Barry said. That's the neighbour.'

'I see.'

Jane never liked it when her brother embarked on ferreting out the answers to what puzzled him, but he had an uncanny instinct for recognizing when intervention was justified. He seemed to attract crime as others attracted runs of good or bad luck. It would be typical of him to run over not just any harmless poodle, but one connected with some sort of mystery.

'How can I find out what happens at the inquest on Tina Willoughby?' he asked now.

'By going to it, I should think,' said Jane.

'No, I don't want to do that.' Patrick did not want to show too much interest. 'I suppose you couldn't pop over?'

'I certainly could not,' said Jane.

Patrick thought of the talkative neighbour. She would be sure to attend; she might have to give evidence of finding the body. He could call on her again. By the time he returned from Stratford-upon-Avon he would have decided on a plan. He said so to Jane.

'Are you going to the theatre already? Has the season begun?' she asked. 'Oh, it must have, I suppose. It's Miranda's birthday soon. Don't forget it, will you?'

Miranda had been born on Shakespeare's birthday, and Patrick approved of her name, though at the time he had said that if she were a boy he hoped he would have been called, if not William, then George, after the saint whose day it was also, rather than, for example, Orlando.

'I'm not planning to go to the theatre,' he said.

II

The third estate agent whom Patrick consulted in Stratford-upon-Avon was the one who had sold a house to Tina Willoughby. It was too late, after he left Jane, for him to get there before their offices closed, but he left Oxford early the next morning and arrived soon after nine-thirty. As he drove out of Oxford through the incoming traffic he gave hearty thanks that living in college saved him from this daily grind; what with the bus lanes, the long one-way detours and the new shopping precincts, Oxford was sadly changed.

He was hoping to bluff the relevant estate agent into providing the information he sought, since he had no authority to ask for it; the news of Tina's death might not have reached them yet, house-buying being, as he knew, a protracted procedure. He had thought of posing as an interior decorator with an appointment to view the place but who had lost the address; however, he decided that he did not look the part. Instead, he said that he was passing through the town on his way home after a week's absence, and had arranged to meet Tina there, but could not remember where it was, adding that he had been unable to contact her on the telephone. In this way he was covered if the agent knew of her death; he would be told, and in the ensuing lamentations the address would certainly be divulged.

How very much simpler things were for the police, he reflected; they had only to ask. But they could not carry out searches and so forth without warrants, when sometimes a lay person could nose his way in and just look about in an innocent manner.

A thin, pale girl gave him the address without demur; she made no mention of the tragedy.

The house was about four miles from Stratford-upon-Avon, in a village that bordered the river. It was thatched, with a lawn running down to the water's edge, and apple trees almost in bud in the garden. He had wondered if the former owner would still be there, but it was empty. If the sale had not been completed there might now be some legal wrangle; it would be tough on the vendor if he were to lose the sale through Tina's death. Patrick prowled around, peering in at the windows. The rooms were low and beamed, the windows leaded. It had been well restored but looked in need of paint; the various plants climbing the walls were overgrown and wanted trimming. The main structure was very old; standing as it did near the bridge over the river it could well have been a pub once, and Patrick allowed himself to imagine that Shakespeare might have called there for some ale.

He pondered how to proceed.

There was a pub in the village, but it was not yet open; however, there was a shop selling groceries two or three hundred yards further on. He entered it, found it to be of the old-fashioned sort with human service behind a counter, and waited patiently for his turn; then he bought a jar of instant coffee and some biscuits, which would always come in handy. As he paid, he said casually:

'I noticed an empty cottage down by the river. It's very pretty. Do you know if it's for sale? I've got a friend who's looking for a place just like that.'

There was instant reaction from everyone in the shop.

'That'll be Pear Tree Cottage, Joss Ruxton's place,' came the first answer.

'Sold, it is. You're too late.'

'A lady from down London way's bought it.'

The answers came from all sides, but the one name registered with Patrick. Joss Ruxton, an actor who had played at the Royal Shakespeare Theatre with notable success for several seasons, was at present in the company at the Fantasy in London and Patrick had seen his performance as Macbeth on the night when Sam's body was found.

'Well, do you know of any other houses round about?' Patrick stuck to his cover.

He was told of one.

'Not in such good order, it isn't,' said someone. 'He was keen on the garden.'

'It's rather overgrown,' Patrick remarked.

'Bound to be. Left without clearing it up, they did.'

'Used to have rare old parties down on the river,' said a stout woman.

'Is his wife an actress too?' asked Patrick.

'She wasn't his wife, dear,' said the woman. 'But ever so sweet.'

Patrick departed at last, having learned that Joss's mistress had left before the end of the season to film in Spain, after which things had not seemed quite the same at Pear Tree Cottage. Joss had gone before the season finished completely with a play in which he had no part. It seemed he owned a house in London too.

Patrick went back to have a more thorough look at the cottage; his interest in it had now been explained and he was unlikely to be challenged if anyone saw him prowling around. Peering through the kitchen window he saw an electric kettle on the drainer, beside a clean, empty milk bottle, and a garden chair, unfolded, in the centre of the room. Someone had been picnicking here: was it Tina? He went into the garage, which seemed to have no lock. There were tyre marks on the dusty floor and a pile of old sacks in a corner.

But there was nothing to show that Sam had ever been there.

PART 5

I

Patrick did not care for the architectural style of the Royal Shakespeare Theatre, but he had spent many happy hours inside it, so, like a *jolie laide*, it charmed him as he walked towards it from the big car park beside Clopton Bridge. He crossed the road and went through the gardens. A few people stood on the river bank looking at the swans, and more were strolling about in front of the theatre.

Patrick's former pupils were employed all over the world in various ways; some taught; some were journalists; some were civil servants, a few were politicians. He had lost track of many, but he remembered that one had a job here behind the scenes in the theatre, though in what capacity he could not recall: publicity, perhaps, or was it to do with finance? Never mind, it did not matter.

He enquired for Denis Vernon at the box office, where no one had heard of him, so they sent him round the side of the building to the office entrance, telling him to try there.

Some minutes later Patrick was being led along echoing stone corridors, past door after door, and at last was deposited in a small office where two girls were typing and a young man with close-cropped hair was talking into a telephone.

It took Patrick a moment to recognize Denis, for when last seen he wore shoulder-length locks; shorn like this he looked startlingly naked.

Denis gestured at Patrick and went on talking animatedly into the telephone about some cheque that had gone astray. The two girls looked up; one looked straight back at her typewriter again, but the other smiled and invited Patrick to sit down. There was one small, frail chair available, its back to the wall, and sitting in it, Patrick's legs stretched almost across the width of the room, which was long and narrow, with a counter running along one side on which the two typewriters rested. Behind Denis, a window overlooked the town; the office was warm and snug: no wonder, with so many people in it, Patrick thought. Photographs of scenes from various past Stratford productions hung on the wall, and he amused himself by trying to identify the players and the plays while he waited. Soon Denis replaced the telephone with a thump and came surging across the room, to the peril of the other occupants. Patrick had forgotten how vigorously he always strode about.

'Well, Patrick, how nice! What are you doing here?' he exclaimed heartily.

'Just passing through,' said Patrick, feeling suddenly fatigued by this exuberance. 'I remembered you were here and thought you might have lunch with me — just a snack in a pub somewhere.'

'I'd love it. As it happens, I'm free today,' said Denis. He glanced at his watch. 'In half an hour? At the—'

Patrick cut him short and named a pub where the beer was famous.

'Jean will show you the way down,' said Denis, and Jean, the more friendly of the two girls, rose to lead him back to the outer world.

Patrick would have enjoyed finding his own way out, with a chance to prowl about in this interesting place, where suddenly you saw a row of costumes on a rack, or another corridor leading off into the unknown fascinations of the backstage theatre. As he followed Jean, who looked good from the rear in her tight trousers, an actor he recognized passed them. He wore the current uniform of dark brown corduroy trousers and waistcoat, over which could be thrown cloak or doublet, which the company had adopted latterly. Jean told him as they went along that this side of the theatre had formerly been dressing-rooms; now most of these were on the river side of the building. That accounted for the long, narrow shape of the office they had just left.

The play tonight was *Othello*, a repeat of the previous year's successful production, though with a different cast. Patrick thought that he might try to pick up a ticket for it; he had seen it last year with Joss Ruxton as Othello and had enjoyed it; the director had steered away from some of the gimmicky tricks which had so enraged faithful Stratford theatregoers in recent years.

Denis arrived at the pub five minutes late. He burst in, almost knocking over a mild youth who was standing by the door drinking a coke.

'Well, Patrick, how's everything?' he cried, and without waiting for an answer went on, 'sorry I hadn't time for you in the office. It's all go, go, you know. Season proper starts soon and there's lots to do.'

'I'm sure there is,' said Patrick. 'What will you drink?'

'It's lucky you found me free today,' said Denis, when they had got their beer. 'Hi, there!' he called to a group on the other side of the room, which was heavily timbered, rather dark, and loaded with atmosphere, some of it genuinely old. His acquaintances across the room waved back.

'Are they theatre people?' Patrick asked. 'Your friends?'

They were. Denis named them for him. They were all connected with the administration; none were actors.

'How long have you been here?' Patrick asked.

'Three years.'

'You must know most people in Stratford by this time?'

'Oh, I wouldn't go so far as to say that,' said Denis modestly. 'There are so many. But a lot, a lot.'

'You like it here?'

'Oh yes. It's alive — exciting,' said Denis.

Patrick could believe it. Although Denis was rather overpowering, his enthusiasm was endearing; Patrick often grew depressed by the negative approach of so many people to their lives and occupations.

'I suppose you're busy with rehearsals now?' he asked.

'Only the first plays,' said Denis. 'They get them together in the last eight weeks — the casting's often not finished till then.'

'So late?'

'That's right. The leading actors are agreed sooner, usually, but not the others. Actors live very much from day to day. They get offered things, and take them, and then aren't available when they're wanted later.'

'You mean suddenly a film part turns up, or something?'

'Yes. Or television — they're gone for ten weeks if they land a series, and perhaps it may lead to another, whereas a season here may not. If someone from television says, "We want you on Wednesday," they'd be mad not to take it.'

'A bird in the hand, you mean.'

'Yes.'

'Must make the producer's job difficult.'

'Oh, it does. There's a lot to be thought of, you know. You want someone for a big part who'll accept a small one in another play, and so on.'

'And I suppose they have to fit in together, as a team?'

'Oh yes.'

Patrick had not realized quite how last-minute it all was. He had imagined that the director sat down a year ahead selecting his cast from the top to the bottom and signing them up then and there. Such eleventh-hour planning would not suit him as a way of life.

'There's a bit of a panic on now, I believe. Chap they'd got for Friar Lawrence in *Romeo and Juliet* later in the year jumped in the Thames last week,' said Denis blithely.

Patrick sat up. Here it was.

'What?' he said.

'Mm. Sam Irwin. Not well known, but a good actor. He's been here before. They wanted him last year, but for some reason he couldn't come.'

'I remember Sam Irwin,' said Patrick. 'Why did he jump in the river?'

'I've no idea. Pressure of life, I suppose,' said Denis.

While they ate thick slices of cold ham and baked potatoes, Patrick discovered that most of the actors lived in lodgings or flats round the district; some of the permanent staff had houses in Stratford; Denis himself had a flat in a new block in the town.

'Have they found anyone to take Sam Irwin's place?' Patrick asked after a while.

'Oh, bound to have,' said Denis. 'They'll have rung round the agents.'

'Had he been up to audition?'

'He wouldn't audition — not someone like him, who's been around for ages. Things aren't done like that here,' said Denis kindly. 'He'd have been chosen and would have accepted — probably all through his agent. He might have come up to arrange about digs or something like that. I don't know. Why?'

'Oh, I was just curious,' said Patrick. 'It seems odd that he should jump in the river when he'd got a season here planned. What else was he going to be?'

'Oh, something or other in *Julius Caesar* — Cinna, was it?'

'Cinna the poet? Or the other one?'

'I don't know.'

'Hm. Cinna the poet came to a sticky end too,' said Patrick.

'Irwin's career does seem to have been rather a stop-go one. Maybe he didn't feel he could cope with the challenge here,' said Denis, with surprising insight. 'He'd have had at least one more part — probably not a very big one — in *Henry V*.'

'You mean he may have got stage fright?'

'Could be.'

Some shock or other had made Sam's heart stop before he could drown. Was it the sudden chill of total immersion, or the terror of being bound and stuffed in a sack? But why should anyone want to tie him up and stuff him in a sack? It all came back to that.

Patrick walked back with Denis to the theatre, with the aim of trying to get a ticket for the evening performance. Just as they arrived, he saw Sergeant Bruce, last seen in Sam's Hammersmith digs, and an older man in plain clothes, leaving the stage door. They got into a large black car and drove away.

So the police had learned of Sam's commitment here and come to enquire about it. And they had come from London, not merely asked for a report from the local force.

He wondered what they had been able to learn. What a pity the case was not a Yard one; then he could have asked Colin.

He decided to postpone *Othello* until another time.

II

It was not at all difficult to discover the name of Sam Irwin's agent. Patrick simply went round to the stage door of the Fantasy Theatre and asked, after driving straight to London from Stratford-upon-Avon. By this time the cast were beginning to come in for the evening performance. The stage doorkeeper telephoned somebody, and a man appeared whom Patrick recognized as the actor playing Malcolm. He supplied the answer straight away, said he was grieved about Sam, and announced that he meant to go to the funeral.

Patrick was glad to find some evidence that Sam had been regarded, if not with affection, at least with esteem, by his colleagues. It was too late to call on the agent now; that must wait. The evening lay blankly ahead, and he thought of Liz. He got into the car and drove to Bolton Gardens, where she lived.

Liz took some time to answer the bell, and he had almost given her up when at last he heard her disembodied voice over the entryphone as he stood on the step outside the old house in which she had a flat. She sounded surprised when she heard who it was below, but bade him enter, and the door unlocked to admit him.

Her flat was on the third floor. It had only two rooms, apart from the bathroom and kitchen, but they were large. Patrick had not been there for some time; there was a comfortable feeling of familiarity, however, as he walked through the door which Liz had left slightly ajar and into the hall, where a vase of daffodils stood on a small table under an old, gilt-framed mirror. Liz appeared at once, wearing a towelling robe.

'I was having a bath when you rang,' she said.

Patrick kissed her. He always did when they met, but chastely. Now he suddenly kissed her a second time, and with more fervour.

She looked surprised, but pleased.

'You look very seductive,' he said.

'Do I?' She laughed, blushed slightly, and added, 'Good.'

It was Patrick's turn to look surprised.

'Are you expecting anyone?' he asked suspiciously.

I should say yes, thought Liz, but she answered truthfully.

'No. I've got a manuscript to read. I was going to spend the evening with it.' Liz was a publisher's editor.

'Come out to dinner instead,' said Patrick, and rather spoiled it by adding, 'to make up for the other evening.'

'All right. Since you press me, I will,' she agreed.

'Oh, Liz, I didn't mean it like that,' said Patrick, aware suddenly of how graceless he sounded. 'What a boor I am.'

It was unlike him to castigate himself.

'Give yourself a drink while I get dressed,' she said, suppressing an impulse to reassure him. 'You know where everything is.'

'Hang on a minute,' said Patrick, putting a hand on her arm as she turned away. Her hair was damp round her small, pointed face, and her eyes were large and dark. There were shadows under them. She looked up at him, and there was an instant when either of them might have drawn back with a laugh or a light remark, but neither did. Patrick kissed her again, and less chastely this time.

After some moments they did move apart and gazed at one another in wonder. Then the habit of years reasserted itself; they both laughed, Patrick released her and the incident was over. Liz disappeared into her room, and Patrick went into her sitting-room considerably shaken.

Watch it, he told himself. Liz'll throw you out if you get those sort of ideas about her; you're a brother figure to her, no more. You can't treat Liz like some other girl; she's vulnerable, and you've known her too long. Besides, you don't want any complications.

When she came back, wearing a long blue skirt and a striped shirt, looking somewhat Edwardian, she behaved as if nothing had happened, sitting in the one armchair and not beside him on the sofa. She seemed composed. While dressing, she had wondered, in some agitation, what mood to adopt, and had decided to play for safety.

The foolish pair sipped their drinks in detached amity.

'Have you any more news about Sam?' Liz asked.

PART 6

I

Patrick drove back to Oxford late that night feeling unsettled. Liz had seemed different. All through dinner he had found himself noticing how their minds dovetailed, how swiftly she picked up an allusion, something he had hitherto taken for granted. And she was nice to look at, sitting opposite him in the candlelight.

They talked about Sam, and Patrick described his visit to Stratford-upon-Avon.

'But if it wasn't suicide, what could have happened?' Liz asked.

'I don't know. No one could have had a motive for murdering him.'

'Professional rivalry? Someone else wanting to be Friar Lawrence?'

'Hardly. He wasn't successful enough for that. Besides, do you think actors really go round killing one another out of professional jealousy? I doubt it.'

'Who'll get his parts now?'

'I've no idea.'

'It must have been an accident. He fell in the river — I don't know — after a few drinks. On his way to the theatre.'

'But the rope marks on his wrists — how do you explain them?'

'Some sex aberration?' hazarded Liz.

'Well — I hadn't thought of that,' Patrick admitted. 'It's possible, I suppose. But Sam — surely not?'

'How can one tell about other people?' Liz asked.

'You thought he wasn't interested, when we met him in Greutz,' Patrick remembered.

'He was nervous of women. Some men are,' said Liz. She hesitated, then plunged on: nothing was altered: this was Patrick, with whom for half her life she had felt free to discuss any subject. 'They're afraid that more may be expected of them than they're prepared — or perhaps able — to offer. An inverted form of conceit, when you think about it. He was a nice man, though. He relaxed, once he was sure no one was trying to trap him.'

'He was very unsure of himself. I realize that now,' said Patrick.

'Yes. Covered it up by fleeing,' said Liz. 'One does, doesn't one—' She let the sentence fade away, looking suddenly embarrassed, and inspected the small posy of flowers arranged on their table.

Patrick regarded her curiously. He knew little about her day-to-day life now. In Austria, where they had met Sam, she had been attracted to one of the men in the group she was with; Patrick had thought her oddly naive at the time, and he knew she had not enjoyed the experience. Had she indulged in more rewarding amorous encounters since then? Looking at her, he could not believe that she had no emotional life, yet he knew very well that many people who would have chosen otherwise were obliged to accept such a condition.

He told her about Manolakis, the poodle, and the death of Tina Willoughby. It broke the tension between them.

'But it's sheer coincidence that this Tina woman was moving to Stratford when Sam was going there. There can't be any connection. Or if there is, the police will find it,' said Liz.

'I suppose you're right. But I do wonder why she killed herself,' said Patrick.

'Why did she want to move to Stratford?'

'Because of her interest in the theatre, the neighbour thought. As Sam was going there so soon there could be a link.'

'How can you find things out about her? Knowing you, I imagine you mean to try,' said Liz.

'Chat casually to someone who knew her — see what comes up in the course of general conversation.' Patrick ignored Liz's sardonic tone.

'Mm. Couldn't you suggest to the police that they should do it?'

'Yes. But if this is a red herring, it's a pity to go stirring things up,' said Patrick.

'I see your point. If something came up at the inquest on Tina to show she knew Sam, the police would automatically follow it up.'

'Yes.'

'But it wouldn't be the same police force, would it? Dealing with both?'

'No, but if something like that was disclosed about Tina, I think London would hear about it,' said Patrick.

'So you'll wait and see what happens?'

'I think so. More or less.'

As they drove back to her flat she commented on the car.

'I like it. Much more dashing than the Rover,' she said. 'What made you choose this?'

He could not tell her that he feared the onset of middle age and sought to enliven his image.

'It's fun to drive,' he said. 'You're close to the road — there's immediate, precise control. Like riding a horse — which I've done quite a bit, though you may find it hard to believe.'

'Is there anything you haven't done, Patrick?' she asked.

'Skin-diving,' he answered at once. 'I'm scared of it.'

The thought of Patrick being scared was disarming.

'I thought you had no nerves,' she said.

'I'm afraid of a lot of things,' he told her. 'Not all of them requiring physical courage.'

He went up with her to the flat, where she made coffee and put on a record. It was Mozart.

'Nice,' he said.

'Yes.'

'The manuscript — the one you were going to read tonight. What is it?'

'Oh — a biography of Florence Nightingale,' she said.

'Any good?'

'Yes, I think so. We'll probably do it.'

'Have you been to Claydon House?'

'No.'

'Neither have I. We should be ashamed of ourselves. It's so close to Oxford.'

'Yes.'

'We could go, of course.'

'Why not?'

The weekend stretched blankly ahead of Liz; she had made no special plans, and to spend time with Patrick, whether or not they visited Florence Nightingale's former home, would be very pleasant.

'We might take Dimitris. He wants to see various sights and I mean to take him to some stately homes. I'll ring you about it,' said Patrick.

'All right,' said Liz, deflated, and decided that she would not, after all, encourage Patrick to stay very much longer this evening.

Driving through the starlit night, Patrick reflected on the evening. In a way, it had ended in a disappointing manner, with no repeat of their warm embrace. Whose fault was that? He tried to work it out. Liz had seemed less approachable, and his own reserve had returned. Perhaps, on the whole, it was just as well.

II

Patrick spent Saturday writing an article about Ben Jonson, and on Sunday he went to lunch with Jane, where he spent the afternoon clipping a hedge with his brother-in-law, and burning the trimmings. Andrew helped them both. Patrick left after tea, pleasantly tired and smelling of wood smoke.

'Patrick's broody,' said Jane, when he had gone.

'Oh?' Michael was used to her speculations about her brother. She often fretted rather crossly about his mode of life.

'Mm. His mind kept wandering. Didn't you notice?'

'Not really. We were just busy with the hedge,' said Michael, who was blessed with an equable disposition and did not go looking for trouble.

'We're very good for him. He's gone back to college now to dine in grandeur,' said Jane. 'If it wasn't for us he'd know nothing about daily life and hedge-cutting. He's got that suicide business on his mind, I suppose. I wish he'd leave it alone.'

'He's been useful, several times.'

'I know. But he finds things out about himself while he's uncovering crimes, and it's not always happy for him,' said Jane.

'Darling, he's a grown man — and he's been a fellow of his college for a good many years now. Don't worry so much about him.'

'I'm not exactly worrying. I just think he compensates in some way for his own personal failures by sorting out other people's,' said Jane.

'Is there anything wrong with that?'

'No, not if it helps all round in the end. But it's vicarious living. Don't you agree?'

'Well—' Michael was not sure. 'Up to a point, perhaps.'

'He likes running home to St Mark's when he's had enough of the real world,' said Jane. 'It's a retreat.'

'Well, at least he makes little forays outside,' he said. 'He doesn't shut himself up the whole time, like some academics.'

'I hope he brings his Greek friend to see us,' Jane said. 'I want to meet him.'

'He probably will,' said Michael. 'He'll want to show him our English way of life.'

Back at St Mark's, Patrick was not dining in the grandeur imagined by Jane, for the college staff were having a rest and the kitchens were closed. He was, in fact, opening a tin of soup and eating biscuits and cheese for his supper. He had forgotten to shop, and the bread in his plastic bin was covered in flourishing mould.

He was delighted when, at nine o'clock, Manolakis rang up to report his business in London concluded and to ask if he might return the next day.

PART 7

I

Manolakis was eager for the experience of travelling by British Rail; trains were not a feature of life in Crete. However, Patrick insisted that he had a call to make in Dean Street and would collect him afterwards.

He parked in Soho near the office of the agent whose address he had been given at the Fantasy Theatre. It was above a pizza restaurant, and strong, cheesy smells filtered up the stairway to the dark passage above, where a glass door bore the name *Leila Waters,* painted in black, and a sign instructed *Enter and Wait.*

Patrick entered.

In a small room with green walls and a cream ceiling, and an unvarnished board floor, three men sat on chain ranged round the sides of the room like patients waiting for the doctor. Two looked despondent, the third desperately alert. None was young. Over their heads were ranged a variety of blown-up photographs, none of which showed a face which Patrick was able to recognize.

A thin girl with frizzed hair and high platform soles sat typing at a desk in the corner.

'She won't see you without an appointment,' was the response when Patrick asked for an audience with Leila Waters.

'Please take her this and ask her if she would be good enough to spare me five minutes,' said Patrick, as he took a card from his wallet and wrote a few words on the back of it.

The girl looked at him suspiciously.

'I'm not an actor. It's about something else,' said Patrick, and felt the atmosphere in the room change as the three waiting men stopped silently registering horror at his effrontery.

'Well, I'll ask,' said the girl. 'But I'm sure she won't see you.'

She disappeared through a chocolate-brown door. Certainly Sam's agent wasted no percentages on the premises, thought Patrick. He sat down, well away from the trio of men. The alert one was fidgeting, twitching his foot up and down and snapping his fingers. Patrick wondered if he was mentally practising some dance routine. The other two men stared into space. As the girl came back, the telephone on her desk rang.

'You're to go in,' she said to Patrick, swinging her hips behind the desk and seizing the receiver while she spoke.

Watched resentfully by the other men, Patrick went through the chocolate-brown door.

A fat, white-haired woman sat behind a scratched desk talking into another telephone. She had stubby fingers with chunky rings on most of them, and her nails were painted blue. The walls here were covered with more photographs, and this time Patrick recognized nearly all the faces. He saw Joss Ruxton, the actor who had played Othello last year at Stratford, and his Desdemona, and a print of Sam taken long ago dressed as Jaques.

'Yes — I know you've an audition on Tuesday, but this would be better for you — eight weeks filming and who knows what might come after that if the film's any damn good. Now, you get along there,' the woman was saying, and she waved a hand at Patrick to sit down.

He did so, watching while she talked on, cajoling and bullying, and eventually reached agreement with her client, after which she slammed down the receiver.

'Now. Three minutes, that's all,' she said, fixing Patrick with a bright blue stare from tiny, deep-set eyes. Her voice was youthful, and her diction crisp; he guessed she had once been on the stage herself.

'Sam's funeral — do you know when it is?' Patrick asked her.

'He can't be cremated — some ban by the coroner. It's on Wednesday at ten,' said Leila Waters. She scribbled something on a piece of paper, tore it from a pad and gave it to him. 'There. That's the cemetery and the name of the undertaker.'

'Thank you,' said Patrick.

'Well, Sam's troubles are over. Pity,' said Leila. 'He had talent.'

'Why didn't he get any further?' Patrick asked.

'It was his own fault. There was that business years ago — you knew about it?'

Sam had been mixed up in a drug scandal; he had been acquitted in court of any complicity in what had gone on but he had had a breakdown, broken a contract, and been out of work for years.

'He needn't have dropped out of sight then,' Leila went on. 'But his nerve went — he wouldn't turn up for auditions, or if he did, he dried — couldn't do a thing. He was almost washed up.'

'What made him keep at it?'

'I did. Told him to stop wallowing in self-pity and get on with it, and found fresh opportunities for him when no other agent would have bothered. I always believed in his ability, but his temperament was too much — it beat him in the end.'

The telephone rang, and she spoke into it again for some minutes. It was a call about finding an actress for a commercial. Patrick listened with interest to the conversation. He thrived on seeing aspects of life so different from his own.

'Stratford,' he said, when Leila had finished. 'Sam was going to be Friar Lawrence and Cinna.'

'Not Cinna — Caesar,' said Leila. 'That could have made him. He might have settled down and become a regular part of the company.'

'Caesar himself, indeed,' said Patrick thoughtfully. Denis had got it wrong.

'Yes. Another actor was picked first, but he couldn't do it in the end — a film part came up, and he took that.'

'So it was offered to Sam? He was already going up there for *Romeo and Juliet?*'

'Yes.'

'He seemed to have no friends,' said Patrick.

'He was a loner. I doubt if anyone ever got close to him,' said Leila. 'I can't help you, if you want to know why he did it. I told the police the same thing.' She reached out for the telephone. 'I've got to find that actress,' she said, and, as Patrick still remained sitting in front of her, added, 'I sent him off several times to audition for really good parts — things he could do on his head if only he'd kept it — but he didn't turn up. You can't keep on indefinitely with someone like that.'

Yet she'd done it: persevered for years, and thought at last that she'd found him a niche where he might take root.

'Nerves?'

'No confidence. Many actors lack it — some of the greatest never get over their nervousness — but the obsession with acting overcomes it. The business is harsh — tough — unless they fight they don't get on. There are hundreds of people with talent and someone unreliable won't be chosen if there's a reliable actor around waiting to grab what's going.'

'So you think he was capable of suicide?'

'He proved it, didn't he? Yet I thought this time he was really looking forward to the season. The run at the Fantasy went well, and he's always liked doing Shakespeare.'

'It seems funny that he lost his nerve about Stratford when he'd done that spell at the Fantasy,' Patrick said. 'I should have thought that was more of a challenge.'

Leila shrugged.

'He'd done Macduff before, in rep. He'd never played Caesar,' she said. 'He's the sort of person who, when they're gone, you forget — it's as if he never was,' she added. 'A negative man.'

'What a terrible epitaph.' Patrick was shocked.

Leila shrugged, impatient for him to leave.

'Had he a drink problem?'

'Not now. In the past.'

'Any enemies?'

'You're joking. He wasn't positive enough. No friends and no foes. Now, you've had far more than three minutes of my valuable time,' Leila said. 'Goodbye.'

She started her telephoning again as Patrick left. The three men in the outer office had been joined by a dark girl. None took the least notice of him; all were absorbed by their own problems.

They were looking for roles to play. But they must have other things too in their lives — lovers — people to whom they related in some fashion. Or did they all come to life only when they were acting?

And what about Sam?

II

Patrick spent the afternoon in the cinema and then met Dimitris Manolakis outside the British Museum, where he had been keeping a tryst with the fragments from the Parthenon.

He had also visited St Paul's and Westminster Abbey with his relations, and he was wearing a new sweater which showed he had visited another tourist mecca.

'I have some news about your dead friend,' said Manolakis. 'You might like to hear it right away.' His English sounded more fluent already, though he must have been speaking Greek with his relations. 'I have been to see the good Colin Smithers this morning and he told me. He knew you would want to know.'

The way Manolakis gambolled about among English verbs was impressive; but Greek ones were so difficult that ours must seem child's play to one who had grown up with those, Patrick reflected.

'The police are satisfied. They think his death was suicide, but he died from failing heart, not drowning. He had been acting out his fantasies.'

'I don't believe it,' said Patrick. 'You mean he tied himself up, acting out some masochistic scheme, and then jumped in the river?'

After a little sorting out of the linguistics of this, Manolakis agreed.

'And he died from fear before he is hitting the water,' he said, letting his tenses slip. 'His arteries were not good.'

'So they're stopping enquiries?'

'That is right.'

'What do you think, Dimitri?'

'I did not know your friend. I cannot judge. These things happen, it is known. Colin has told me of many unhappy cases.'

'But the shreds of sacking under his fingers — what about them?'

'Perhaps for some time beforehand he is tying himself inside a sack?'

If this was a case of some sort of perversion, it was possible. Inconsequentially, Patrick remembered the pile of sacks in the garage at the empty cottage near Stratford-upon-Avon.

'I'm not at all happy about this,' he said. 'Let's go and ask Liz what she thinks about it.'

'Liz? Who is Liz?'

'She's a friend of mine — she knew Sam,' he said. 'And there's a whole lot more, Dimitri,' and he told him about Tina Willoughby.

'But you have no proof that this lady knew Sam?'

'Not yet.'

Manolakis had heard from Colin about Patrick's uncanny instinct for sensing trouble. His nose, Colin had called it, and the Greek had seen proof of it himself in the past. It was a faculty he too possessed, and he respected it in another; the owner of it would worry away at a problem until he solved it, even if it took years.

'If it was so, you will find out,' he said.

They had hit the rush hour, and it took some time to get from Bedford Square to Bolton Gardens. Manolakis did not mind; the London crowds fascinated him. He had never seen so many people herded together. Athens was a great and bustling city, but the population of London equalled that of the whole of Greece; it was a sobering reflection. He looked benevolently at the convoys of large red buses and the hurrying citizens; he had no responsibility for any of them, he was merely an observer.

Patrick, meanwhile, was wondering what had made him think of consulting Liz. After all, they had met only a few days before. She would be very surprised to see him again so soon.

She was, and did not hide it; she also looked pleased. She had only just got back from the office when they arrived.

She gave them drinks and asked Manolakis how he was enjoying his visit, listening with interest to his answers. She had never been to Greece.

'Oh, but you must go!' Manolakis exclaimed. 'You must take her, Patrick,' he cried. 'All English people are loving Greece.'

'Yes, well—' Patrick looked uneasy. He and Liz had met by chance in Greutz; they had never started out on holiday together. He looked at her and was relieved to see her eyes were sparkling and she looked amused. Where had she been on holiday last year, he wondered, never having thought about it before; and more important, with whom?

'About Sam,' he said, to put his thoughts in order, and told her that Manolakis had propounded her own theory.

'It must have been something like that, surely, Patrick,' she said. 'One finds it hard to accept this sort of thing when it happens to someone one knows. It's so sad to think they were so unhappy.'

'His lack of success seemed to be mostly his own fault,' Patrick said, and related what Leila Waters had told him.

'Dimitris and I might call on Tina Willoughby's neighbour on our way home,' he said.

'What excuse will you offer?' Liz asked.

'None. I shall tell the truth — that I was passing and was curious to know how the inquest went. It's always better to stick to the truth. Damn it, I did kill her wretched dog,' said Patrick. 'We'll be going to Stratford anyway, so I can have another look around Pear Tree Cottage then. You do want to go to Stratford-on-Avon, Dimitri, don't you?'

'Ah — that is the home of William Shakespeare. Yes, I like it very much. What is it to be seen? *The Merchant of Venice?* I have studied him.'

'They're not doing that just now,' said Patrick. 'It's *Othello* again this year.'

Perhaps, for a Greek, a play with a less controversial background than the troubled island of Cyprus might be a better choice, but Manolakis appeared unconcerned.

'I would like to see that,' he said.

He did not mind what he saw or where he went; these English friends were warm and kind; where was the well-known British aloofness? He had yet to meet it.

'You will come too?' he said to Liz.

She was startled, and looked at Patrick.

'Please,' said Manolakis, and then was inspired. 'It will be very happy for me if you are both my guests — I buy the tickets. How can it be done?' He was delighted at having found a way to return some hospitality, typically forgetting that Patrick had stayed with him in Crete and the debt was quite the other way. 'You will come, Elizabeth?' He gave each syllable of her name its full value.

Why not, thought Liz. Did Patrick want her to accept? His expression did not reveal what he felt, but it would be silly to make an issue of it; she went with him to the theatre two or three times a year, and afterwards he always quietly forgot her till the next time. This would be merely another such occasion. She would like to see *Othello* at Stratford.

'Thank you, Dimitri. I would like it very much,' she said.

'We may not be able to get tickets at short notice,' Patrick warned.

'You sometimes can at the start of the season,' said Liz. 'We can try. When shall we go? I might be able to get away early on Friday, but otherwise it would have to be Saturday.'

'Let's ring them up,' said Patrick. 'It may be a different play each night.'

Liz had a programme for the first weeks of the season. From that, they saw that *Othello* would be performed on Friday, and also on Saturday for the Birthday performance. They explained to Manolakis that the anniversary of Shakespeare's birthday was always celebrated.

'We won't get in to that. It will be booked up for the important guests,' said Patrick.

'Well, let's try for Friday, then,' said Liz. She was about to make the telephone call herself, automatically, but something stopped her. 'There's the telephone, Patrick,' she said. 'You ring them up.'

He gaped at her. She sounded so bossy; just like Jane. But he rang up the theatre and was able to book three good stalls seats for the Friday performance; the tickets had just been returned.

PART 8

I

'She is a lovely woman, your Elizabeth,' said Manolakis as they drove away. 'She is your mistress?'

'Good heavens, no!' exclaimed Patrick. 'Nothing like that.'

'But why not? Or you will marry — she is not married, is she?'

'She's divorced. Her husband was — her marriage was unhappy — they parted years ago,' said Patrick, feeling flustered at this inquisition.

'You like her.'

'Very much,' said Patrick.

'Well, then, it is natural — the one or the other,' said Manolakis in his direct, Greek way.

'It's not as easy as that,' said Patrick. 'You Greeks, with your warm sunshine and your blue skies — these things seem simpler to you.'

'Take her to Greece, then, Patrick, and it will be simple for you,' said Manolakis.

Patrick was so stupefied by this conversation that he drove in silence for the next six miles while Manolakis admired the countryside.

'Perhaps she has some other lover,' the Greek said after a while.

'Who? Liz?'

'Yes. She is attractive. It must be so.'

The very notion was enough to make Patrick lose his concentration and drive without proper care. He scowled at the road ahead; if Manolakis was right, the fellow might be with her now. What a thought! Patrick gripped the steering-wheel tightly and pushed the car on faster, driving the loathsome idea out of his mind.

Liz, in fact, spent a solitary evening after they had gone, listening to a concert on Radio Three.

When they reached the place where Patrick had hit the dog, he turned off across the common.

Although it was evening now, it was still light, and a few people were strolling about. Some had dogs with them. Several cars were drawn in off the road and parked under the trees. They passed houses which drew surprised and admiring comments from Manolakis. It must all seem very strange to his alien eyes, Patrick supposed. Parts of England were still lovely, despite motorways, flyovers, tower blocks and industrial complexes. He must not let this business about Sam obsess him so much that he failed to take Manolakis around the country; he had planned to show him Devon and Cornwall, and offer Wales or Scotland — even both.

He slowed down and took a left turn along a rough, unsurfaced lane. They passed several houses, then reached the approach to Strangeways. Patrick stopped the car and opened the door.

'Let's walk up the road a little,' he said.

The track petered out past Strangeways and became a footpath over the common. They followed it through some trees and into a clearing on the other side. Standing there, they could see a light on in the house where Tina Willoughby had died.

'I wonder who's in there,' said Patrick.

'The dead lady's family,' said Manolakis.

'There was no one here when I called before,' said Patrick. 'And the neighbour didn't mention a family.'

'She must have someone.' It seemed obvious to Manolakis.

It did not follow. Sam had not.

'Well, we can't ring and ask,' said Patrick There were limits to what he could bring himself to do in the interests of research.

'There is no need.' Manolakis put a hand on Patrick's arm.

A gate in the hedge surrounding Strangeways had opened, and a girl in jeans and an anorak came out. She walked off across the common, head down, unaware of them.

Was she a daughter of the dead woman?

'Let's chat up the neighbour,' he said, and had to explain the idiom.

II

Lettie Barry was drinking a large gin when the doorbell rang. She set it down to open the door, and when she saw Patrick and Manolakis outside, she at once invited them in. Her husband was at home now, and he hospitably offered them drinks.

'I hope we haven't interrupted your dinner,' said Patrick, who in fact did not mind at all.

'We're just going out — we always go out to dinner on Mondays,' said Lettie Barry. 'I get so exhausted doing the washing.'

Was there so much? Surely she was mechanized? It was the sort of house that must have machines for everything. Perhaps she had six children; but there were no signs of any.

'We saw a light on next door. We wondered who was there,' said Patrick, coming straight to the point.

'It's Tessa Frayne — you know, the niece,' said Lettie, still assuming Patrick to be a friend of Tina's.

'Ah yes,' said Patrick, and waited to learn more.

'She inherits everything,' Lettie went on. 'Well — it's really only the house, since Tina's alimony stops with her death. And not this one, either — the new people move in any day now, and Tessa has to give possession. It was all signed and sealed, so it must go ahead. Tessa's decided to throw up her job and live at the Stratford house. She's going to take in lodgers — folk from the theatre, she says.'

'Well!' exclaimed Patrick, since he must make some sort of comment. 'What was she doing?'

'Some secretarial thing. I don't remember what. She's given it up without a qualm, it seems.'

'I suppose she's pretty upset, though.'

'A bit, of course — it was a shock, and it's tragic — but she wasn't close to Tina. Just saw her from time to time in a casual way.'

'The inquest,' Patrick murmured.

'Suicide while the balance of the mind was disturbed,' said Lettie promptly. 'Tessa didn't know of any reason, unless it was the move, but I thought Tina was looking forward to that. The doctor said he'd been treating her for nerves — she was having tranquillizers — and in the past he'd prescribed sleeping pills, though not recently. There were some empty bottles in the bathroom.'

'She was highly strung,' said Hugo Barry, making his first contribution to the discussion. 'Wouldn't you agree?'

Patrick knew that now he must confess.

'In fact, I never met her. I ran over her dog — that poodle — she was already dead at the time, it seems,' he said.

Both the Barrys looked surprised at this, but Hugo, at least, did not condemn Patrick.

'Tiresome little thing,' he remarked. 'Always yapping.'

'It might have caused a serious accident, running out into the road as it did,' said Patrick. Not overfond of dogs himself, except for certain individual ones, he was about to say they could be a great nuisance when his glance lighted on a small bundle by the hearth: a chihuahua wearing a woollen jacket.

Hugo Barry noticed Patrick looking at the dog, and gazed fixedly at his own drink. He showed them to the door when they left shortly afterwards.

'Tina wasn't a cold sort of person,' he said abruptly to them, in the hall. 'I wouldn't want you to get the wrong impression of her.' He paused. 'It was better she moved. And she'd taken up with this actor fellow — I don't know his name.' He gave a wry smile. 'Maybe he's married too.'

'Well!' exclaimed Patrick when they went out to the car. 'What do you make of that, Dimitri?'

Dimitris Manolakis was clicking his tongue against his teeth and smiling.

'Patrick, you have such a — I do not know how to say it — people tell you what they are thinking. No wonder you do not marry — the world is for you — you can choose what you like.'

Patrick felt embarrassed at all this personal speech. He changed the subject. Tina would keep — or the circumstances surrounding her death would.

'We'll have dinner in Thame,' he said. 'There's a famous pub there — someone wrote a book about it once.' He started the car. 'Well, at least you're seeing some British homes and meeting some British people. I wonder what sort of impression you're getting of the nation.'

'Quite good,' said Manolakis, nodding his head. 'Quite good.'

PART 9

I

'I shall have to go in the back,' said Liz with resignation. 'I'm smaller than you, Dimitri, and anyway you must sit where you can see the countryside.'

They were standing in the quadrangle of St Mark's and surveying Patrick's car, which had room in the rear for only a child or a gnome.

'I do not like this for you, Liz,' said Manolakis solemnly.

'Well, let's go in my car,' said Liz. She had arrived in Oxford soon after four, in her old Triumph Herald, 'It's cramped too, but not as much as yours, Patrick. You can spread yourself out in the back. Dimitri must be in front.'

It was decided. Patrick gave in with fair grace. He climbed into the back of the Triumph and arranged his legs as best he could behind the front seats. From this position he had an uninterrupted view of the two dark heads in front of him as their owners chatted eagerly all the way through north Oxford and out on to the Woodstock road. Liz had not been to Oxford since the controversial traffic amendments; she was astonished at the street closures and the bus lanes, and remarked upon them to Patrick, who, because the engine was rather noisy, found it hard to hear what she said. After a while Liz stopped trying to talk to him.

'Did you like Devonshire?' she asked Manolakis.

He and Patrick had spent the week in the West Country, and had been across the Severn Bridge into Wales. Manolakis expounded at length on the delights of their tour; he had enjoyed walking on Dartmoor and looking at the Atlantic from Land's End.

Liz was a good driver, and her old car still had some zip left, Patrick had to admit as he crouched behind while Manolakis compared the wild ponies he had seen with the sheep in Crete. He interrupted the dialogue in front to explain about Blenheim Palace as they came into Woodstock. Liz broke into his account of the first Duke of Marlborough's exploits to tell Manolakis that Sir Winston Churchill was born at Blenheim.

'You can see this palace?' he asked.

'Yes, but we haven't time now,' said Liz. 'In fact there are lots of large houses in this part of the world one can look at.'

'You have so many dukes?' asked Manolakis.

'They don't all belong to dukes,' Liz said. 'There's a lovely one near here where they have all sorts of conferences to do with various problems — Sir Winston stayed there at weekends during the war — it belongs to some sort of trust. Have you been to Ditchley Park, Patrick?' she asked, over her shoulder.

He had not.

'Or Woburn Abbey?'

'No. I don't want baboons on my bonnet,' said Patrick. 'You have to go through a jungle to get to the house.'

'No, you don't,' said Liz. 'The wild life park is quite separate. I'd love to see the house.'

'I'd quite like to see the Canalettos,' Patrick admitted.

'What is this Woburn?' asked Manolakis, so Liz told him about the home of the Duke of Bedford, now handed over to his son.

'There are roundabouts and sideshows,' said Patrick, shuddering.

'There are lions and tigers?' asked Manolakis, his face alight, like a child's. 'I have never seen these. Can we go there?'

Liz, catching Patrick's eye in the driving mirror, saw a look of horror on his face.

'You probably don't have many in Greece,' she said. 'I'll take you, Dimitri.'

'You need not come, Patrick, if it is not your thing,' said Manolakis, who had just learned this expression. 'Liz and I will be happy alone.'

'I'm sure you will,' said Patrick sourly.

'Dimitri, it's very good for us to have visitors from other countries. It makes us realize what treasures we have here,' said Liz earnestly. 'We don't always bother to go and see them unless we have people to show them to.'

'It is the same for us,' said Manolakis generously, and patted her knee.

Patrick leaned forward, inserting his head into the front of the car between the two seats, determined to break up this intimate atmosphere.

'Sam's funeral, Liz. You managed to go?'

'Yes. I took some flowers.'

Patrick had wanted to go to it, but that would have meant interrupting Manolakis's tour to come back to London. Liz had heard about his dilemma when he telephoned to make the arrangements for the weekend, and had offered to go.

'Who was there?' he demanded now.

'Hardly anyone. I was so glad I'd gone. It was awful, really. Utterly bleak.'

'No family turned up?'

'No. There were two men I'm quite sure were policemen — they looked like them, anyway — sorry, Dimitri, no offence meant. They weren't a bit like you, in fact — they were large and solid. And there was a young man whom I spoke to; he was from the Macbeth company. That's all.'

'Just the four of you?'

'Yes. And the undertaker's men lurking about. It was so sad.'

The idea of this dismal farewell appalled Manolakis; Greeks ordered these things differently. He looked shocked.

'So it's not much help to you,' Liz went on.

'Did you look at the flowers?' Patrick asked.

'Yes. Apart from the ones I took, there were some from the Fantasy Theatre — the whole cast, it said. That was all.'

'Hm. Well, you're right — it doesn't give us any new information about his personal life,' said Patrick.

'No. But you'll look up that girl tomorrow, won't you? The one who's got that house up here — she'll have moved by now, won't she?' Liz asked.

'Tessa Frayne. Yes.' Patrick might learn something about her aunt's life from the girl. 'You two needn't come,' he said. 'You can go and goggle at Shakespeare's Birthplace or something.'

'That's a good idea. I'd like that, wouldn't you, Dimitri?' Liz said.

'With you, Liz, I would like anything,' said Manolakis, treating her to an ardent look from his large, dark eyes.

And to crown this exhibition, the play they were to see tonight was one of the most poignant tales of the power of jealousy ever created, Patrick thought, and he withdrew from them, back to the limits of his seat once more. Well, Manolakis would not be in England for long, and he certainly did not want the pair of them getting in his way while he talked to Tessa.

Stratford-upon-Avon, when they reached it, was preparing for Shakespeare's birthday, which would be celebrated the next day, though the actual anniversary came on the 23rd of April. In recent years the festival had been held on the nearest Saturday. Flagpoles were fixed in the streets, and a huge marquee stood in the gardens beyond the theatre.

'The ambassadors from various nations come and parade through the streets,' said Patrick. 'And they have a great luncheon, with speeches and so on.'

'Will some Greek people be here?' Manolakis enquired.

'I suppose so.'

Manolakis was pleased to hear it.

It had been decided that the evening must be made complete for Manolakis with dinner at the theatre after the performance. Patrick went to make sure of their table, leaving

Liz to show Manolakis the photographs of leading actors and actresses in the great roles which adorned the walls of the building. When he came back to them, they were beside the fountain looking at the five studies of Dame Peggy Ashcroft over their heads. They seemed to be standing very close together. Patrick hurried down the stairs to join them.

The stage, when they went into the auditorium, was set with a few pillars representing Venice. About them, the audience rustled with the air of eager anticipation that heralds an exciting theatrical experience. Manolakis was at once aware of the special atmosphere of this place.

'I shall sit between you both,' said Liz, and slid into place with one of them on either side of her, immediately turning to Manolakis to make sure that he knew what was going to happen in the first act of the play, so that he would not get lost when he heard language that would not be easy for him to follow.

Patrick was isolated again. He leafed through the expensive programme with which the management guided their patrons through the history of the play. Usually, when he came here, he simply took a free cast list from the slot on a pillar where they were provided, reckoning that he knew much more about all the plays than anyone involved either with the production or the programmes, but he had bought them each one tonight. There was plenty to read, he found, and it occupied him while Liz and Manolakis talked, but soon he grew restive and looked about him again.

At the side of the dress-circle, in a set of box seats, four men sat together. One had strikingly white hair and a lean profile; the others were younger, one with long hair and the other two neatly trimmed.

'Who's that up there?' Patrick turned to Liz, interrupting her tête-à-tête. 'That chap with white hair. Is he an actor? I know his face.'

Liz looked up at the men in the box.

'It's Ivan Tamaroff,' she said. 'The pianist.'

'That Russian, you mean? The one who came over?'

'Yes — years ago now. He's marvellous,' said Liz, who loved classical music and went to a great many concerts.

'Who are those men with him?'

'I've no idea. I don't recognize any of them,' she said.

As she spoke, viols struck up behind the stage. Slowly the lights dimmed. Liz and Patrick forgot about Manolakis, and indeed about everything as Roderigo and Iago entered, and before them began the build-up of circumstantial evidence that would end, some three hours later, in tragedy.

II

By the interval, Manolakis had become muddled with the plot, so they took their drinks out on to the terrace overlooking the river while they unravelled it for him.

'It is so clever. All those small things which make for suspicion,' he said.

'Envy and jealousy,' said Liz. 'Self-perpetuating evils.'

'What is envy? What is jealousy?' asked Manolakis. 'I think they are the same.'

'Not quite,' said Patrick. 'Iago and Roderigo are envious: Othello is jealous. It's a terrifying play. So much disaster from such a small start.'

They leaned on the parapet and looked down at the water. Two swans swam past, not too haughty to look up at the humans hoping for crumbs. Patrick thought of Sam's hand, white in the dark waters of the Thames. But there was nothing sinister to be seen here, just some weed in the water.

'It is very nice here,' said Manolakis. 'No bodies in this river, Patrick.'

'Not tonight, anyway,' said Patrick. The Avon must, he thought, claim its share.

'There's violence all round us, isn't there?' said Liz, with a wave of her hand that took in the peaceful-seeming playgoers now taking refreshment around them. 'Just under the surface, I mean. People can become primitive when what they value is at stake.'

'Or in pursuit of their desires,' said Patrick. 'Power, for example.'

'Like Iago.'

'Yes. And other seekers of power.'

They thought, in their individual ways, of tyrant regimes, student militants, and in Liz's case of more personal threats, and were silent.

A little distance from them, Ivan Tamaroff and his companions were also looking at the water. The pianist was talking animatedly, gesturing with both hands.

'A free man,' said Manolakis. 'It is good to travel, Patrick. I am enjoying my journey very much. Without you, I could not have done all these things.'

'It's my pleasure, Dimitri,' said Patrick. 'You were so kind to me in Crete. I stayed with you for many days, and you treated me like a brother,' he added, with Greek extravagance of expression. 'Dimitri's wife is an angel,' he said to Liz. Let her not forget that the Greek was married.

'Ah yes. She is a good woman,' said Manolakis.

A bell warned that the interval was coming to its end, and they turned to move back into the theatre. Manolakis took Liz by the elbow and guided her along. Patrick followed, his broad shoulders slumping as he felt suddenly superfluous. But Liz spoke to him as they took their seats.

'Now for that bothersome handkerchief,' she said. 'It's very good, Patrick. He's a wonderful Othello.'

'Yes — better than Joss Ruxton was — very different,' Patrick agreed.

Manolakis was sitting forward, gazing at the stage, eager not to lose a syllable of the next act.

'He isn't really missing much,' Liz said.

'No,' said Patrick, and added, dourly, 'He doesn't, ever.'

'He's very nice,' said Liz.

Patrick did not want to see Liz hurt again by her tendency to be swayed by passing fancies; thinking it was for her protection, not his own, he took her hand and clasped it firmly as Iago and Othello entered.

By the end of the play all three of them were wrung out with emotion. Manolakis had missed none of the poignancy; Patrick and Liz, hanging on every familiar word, were borne along by the tide of the disaster. At the end, they could not speak, and at first could not come down to earth enough even to applaud.

As they filed slowly out, Liz slipped her hand into Patrick's again, and that, suddenly, seemed important.

PART 10

I

Tessa Frayne was standing on some steps arranging plates along a beam when Patrick called at Pear Tree Cottage the following day. It was a fine morning and the sun was pouring in through the latticed windows. She was aware of a shadow falling across the threshold of the opened front door and turned to see a tall man, broadly built, with thick rimmed spectacles and straight dark hair, standing there.

'Miss Tessa Frayne?' he asked.

She thought he must be yet another lawyer; he looked that sort of man.

'My name's Patrick Grant. I came to ask about your aunt. I was so sorry to hear about her death,' he said.

Tessa climbed down from her ladder.

'I'm interrupting you. Here, let me,' said Patrick. He took the remaining plates from her, reached up, and arranged them neatly without need of the steps.

'Oh — thanks,' said Tessa, somewhat taken aback. 'What about my aunt?'

'We never met, but we had a mutual acquaintance.' It was fair to describe the poodle thus. 'It must have been a dreadful shock for you.'

'I haven't really taken it in yet,' Tessa admitted. 'It's only just happened and look at me as a result.'

'"Thou art translated,"' Patrick murmured, and added, 'You'll stay here?'

'Wouldn't you, if you'd the chance?' she asked. 'It's everybody's dream cottage.'

'It's certainly charming.' Patrick was stooping to avoid resting his head against the ceiling. 'Your aunt never lived here.'

'No. It makes the whole thing so hard to understand, doesn't it? Why should she kill herself?'

'Do you know why she was moving up here? She was fond of the theatre, I believe.'

'Yes, that's true. It may have been the reason. Or she may have wanted to be further from London. Or there may have been complications. I really don't know.'

Complications: Hugo Barry. If they had been having an affair and he had ended it, she might have wanted to get away.

'After all,' Tessa went on, 'if you haven't got to live somewhere for a particular reason, how do you choose?'

'It's meant a big decision for you, hasn't it? You made your mind up pretty quickly,' said Patrick.

'Well, the other house had to be cleared. I couldn't mess things up for the buyers by squatting in it,' said Tessa. 'I'm really only a custodian here until probate's been granted.'

This was true, but she could have sent everything to store while she took stock.

'Did your aunt know Sam Irwin?' Patrick asked.

'Sam Irwin? Who's he?'

'He was an actor, but he's dead. He was found in the Thames about a fortnight ago.'

Tessa looked startled.

'I've never heard of him. Should I have?'

'If you were to see a photograph of him you'd probably recognize him,' said Patrick.

'I never heard Tina mention him, but that doesn't mean she didn't know him,' said Tessa. 'Why do you ask?'

Patrick looked at the porcelain she had been unpacking from the removal men's wrappings.

'He wanted his friends to have various mementoes,' he invented. 'But he didn't leave a list. Someone thought your aunt was a friend of his.'

'There might be letters — something like that — or a photograph. I haven't had time to go through everything yet. There are various papers in her desk.'

Tessa crossed to a walnut bureau which stood in a corner and opened a drawer. She took out a bundle of papers.

'There are some photographs here. Would you like a quick look?' she said. 'But it doesn't matter now, as Tina's dead.'

'You should have something instead. There were a lot of records. You might like some of them.'

'Well — Tina wasn't particularly keen on music, but I am — most sorts,' said Tessa. 'However, I don't see why I should be given anything. I didn't know this poor man. Here,' she handed her bundle to him. 'Have a look among these and see if he's there, if you want to.'

She settled him down with the heap of envelopes full of old photographs, and resumed her own unpacking, looking rather pensive. Patrick's queries had raised questions in her mind, he saw. He began looking through snapshots of people quite unknown to him. There were various lean, dark men, and some were so indistinct that they might have been anyone, not excluding Sam. He queried one, and learned he was a painter. Then, among the pile, he came to a collection of old theatre programmes, and in several of them he saw Sam's name. They covered productions with touring companies, and even the recent Playhouse season in Oxford.

'It doesn't prove they were friends,' Tessa objected, when shown these.

'No.'

'I wouldn't like to accept anything of his unless we were really sure. It wouldn't be right,' said Tessa.

'"Oh upright judge,"' said Patrick. 'No, of course you wouldn't,' he added, as she looked at him in surprise. 'You might find some letters later, when you're sorting other things. Would you get in touch with me if you do?'

'Yes, if you like. Anything signed Sam,' she said.

'Please.' He rose to go. 'Here's my address,' he added, producing a card. 'Can I do anything for you while I'm here? Shift something bulky, for instance?' He wanted an excuse to see more of the house, although he could think of nothing he might learn thereby.

'No, it's all right, thanks. Some friends are coming this afternoon — they're watching the Birthday procession this morning.'

So were Liz and Manolakis. Patrick had left them in the town and driven over in Liz's car. They had spent the night in Chipping Camden.

'Sure?' he asked Tessa.

'Well — there is that enormous suitcase to go upstairs. It's full of sheets and things,' she said, pointing to one that was almost as big as a trunk. 'I forgot about it, while the removal men were here. It was difficult to decide about everything.'

She seemed to have done pretty well, all the same, Patrick thought. He picked up the case.

'Right,' he said. 'Where do you want it?'

On her instructions, he took it into one of the bedrooms where there was a huge old oak press, heavily carved, in a corner.

'How did you get that upstairs?' he marvelled, for the staircase was narrow and twisting.

'I didn't. It was here. I think it goes with the cottage,' she said. 'One feels the place was built round it — it's big enough to be a priest's hole in itself. It'll hold all the spare sheets and blankets and so on.'

As they returned downstairs, Patrick remembered what he had seen through the window on his previous visit.

'What's the kitchen like? Modern or Tudor?' he asked.

'See for yourself.'

She waved a hand and he peered in. It was up-to-date, fitted with a stainless steel sink and formica worktops. On the drainer stood a kettle similar to the one he had seen there before. Various packets and tins stood about, among them an open packet of Earl Grey tea.

'Tina must have been camping here,' Tessa volunteered. 'There was a camp bed and some deck chairs and a sleeping bag here, and the kettle and some tea, and a few other things. She probably came to arrange about carpets and so on. But you don't really need carpets on these floors.'

Indeed, upstairs Patrick had noticed the huge, wide boards in the bedrooms, great oaken planks. Downstairs, the floors were all stone flags.

'Odd that they both committed suicide,' Tessa said slowly, walking with Patrick to the door. 'Do you think — if she did know this Sam person — it could have been the reason she killed herself?'

'I was wondering about that, yes,' said Patrick.

'Why did he do it?'

'I don't know.'

'It must be terrible if someone you're in — you're very fond of does that. And you haven't realized that they're desperate, perhaps. Or you think there's something going between you and there isn't.'

'It must, indeed.'

A perceptive, as well as a decisive young woman, Patrick reflected.

'I'll go through those papers as soon as I can,' she said. 'It doesn't matter a bit about the keepsake for me, but you want to know about your friend, don't you?'

'Yes.'

'And I'd quite like to, too, in a way. It would provide a reason,' said Tessa. 'They might have had some sort of pact. But then you'd expect them to do it together, wouldn't you?'

'It could all be some sad misunderstanding between them,' Patrick said, thinking of the waste in Romeo and Juliet.

'She was very nervy. She'd been pretty depressed at one time — on tranquillizers and anti-depressant drugs. That's why I thought it might have been an accident. But apparently she'd taken so many pills that it couldn't have been. No one could have done that by mistake.'

'Her divorce,' Patrick tried.

'Oh, that was ages ago.'

'No children?'

'No. I don't know why not.'

'She was your mother's sister?'

'Yes.'

'Your mother's alive?'

'Very much so. She lives in Dorset. My father's a farmer. Tina was always more one for the merry life and so on, but coming back here was a bit like going back to country life. In a way.'

Only in a way, thought Patrick, if she meant to involve herself with the theatre, but no one knew if that was her plan.

'What did her husband do?'

'He makes motor cars in Coventry. He's got another wife — traded Tina in for a newer model, you could say.'

'Is that what she thought?'

'I'd guess so. That's why she tried so hard to grab someone else. Scared them off, if you ask me.'

That didn't sound as if she would be Sam's sort of person.

'Maybe she wasn't a good picker?' he suggested. He had sometimes thought it about himself.

'Or didn't meet the right person at the right time. There's always that. Still, it's all a gamble, isn't it?' said Tessa.

'What did your aunt do with her time?' Patrick asked. The dead woman was not at all real to him. She had owned some good bits of furniture and some charming ornaments. Various pictures were stacked against the wall of the living-room; he had not looked at them, but from what he had seen of her possessions her taste was good, and she was no pauper. 'She had no career, had she?'

'Not now. She did work in an antique shop once, but she gave it up. She took her poodle for walks — went shopping — had her hair done. That sort of thing. Sounds awful, doesn't it?' said Tessa cheerfully.

It did.

'No satisfying occupation? No hobby?'

'I think she liked the antique shop. I don't know why she gave it up.'

Patrick nodded at the pictures, whose backs faced them.

'Was she keen on art? Are those any good?'

'I shouldn't think so. Have a look at them.'

They were oil paintings of dark, moorland landscapes. At any minute Heathcliff or Cathy would come marching into view, Patrick thought, inspecting the sixth one. He tapped the back of it; it sounded very solid.

'Hm,' he said.

'Pity, isn't it? I might have sold them for thousands of pounds,' said Tessa. 'As it is, I'll be lucky if I can give them away.'

'They're certainly not up to much,' Patrick said. 'But I expect someone will buy them. Well, thank you for putting up with me. We'll meet again.'

'Yes.' Tessa walked with him to the gate. 'There were a lot of people at Tina's funeral,' she said. 'She was cremated. They were mostly neighbours. They were truly shocked, I think. But I wonder if any of them were really fond of her. If they were, you'd think they'd have realized she was desperate.'

'It doesn't always show,' Patrick said.

'Perhaps not.'

Tessa turned to go back to the cottage, then hesitated.

'There was something else rather odd,' she said. 'It came up at the inquest. My aunt was nervous at night — she always put the chain up on the door. That night she didn't, and the door wasn't bolted. It was just shut on the Yale.'

'What did the coroner think about that?' Patrick asked. He remembered Lettie Barry's comment on the same thing.

Tessa shrugged.

'If she was upset enough to commit suicide, she wouldn't bother about locking up,' she said.

She might have wanted to be found before it was too late, Patrick thought, as he drove away; or someone might have been with her — someone who often visited her at night and who had let the dog out inadvertently, perhaps while slipping out himself and pulling the door shut after Tina had unsuspectingly swallowed the fatal dose of pills.

PART 11

I

'I couldn't very well steal it,' Patrick said.

'It would be easy if you were a policeman,' mourned Manolakis. 'You would have the right — and to test all the other things, also.'

While they ate ham rolls in the garden of a pub by the river, Patrick had told him and Elizabeth about the packet of Earl Grey tea he had seen at Pear Tree Cottage. It might easily, he propounded, bear Sam's fingerprints, for he held the theory that it was Sam who had been camping at the cottage.

'Why should he want to?' Liz asked. 'He was acting in London — he couldn't have spent many nights there, anyway. And you've no proof yet that they knew one another.'

'Maybe he stayed there while he looked for digs. Maybe he meant to do a bit of painting for Tina,' said Patrick. 'And another thing — those paintings weren't right. Tina's other things were good — even the valueless ones were in good taste. But the pictures were awful.'

'Perhaps she bought them on spec, hoping they'd come into vogue later and be worth a fortune. Things do happen like that. Like McGonagal,' said Liz, and had to explain to Manolakis about the poet.

'It's the only explanation, I suppose,' said Patrick.

'I think this is one of your hares, Patrick. Lots of people like Earl Grey tea. I do — don't you?'

'Yes.' She was right, and someone with Tina's tastes might be expected to do the same. 'Let's forget it now. Have you two enjoyed yourselves?'

They had had a happy morning. They had watched the Morris dancers, and had had a good view of the procession and the unfurling of the flags, even finding the Greek one. Liz had been able to identify many of the distinguished guests; besides the official representatives from different countries there were actors, writers, and even an American senator. Manolakis felt satisfactorily caught up in the excitement of the occasion.

'It is a great British festival,' he said.

He was right, they supposed, though neither Liz nor Patrick would ever have described it as one.

'Well, what shall we do now? Run round the other Shakespearian shrines or go somewhere else?' asked Patrick. 'Dimitri, what would you like to do?'

'I am at your commands,' said Manolakis.

'There's such a crowd — let's get out of the town and have a spin round the Cotswolds,' said Liz. 'It's a famous part of England, Dimitri, and on a day like this it will be beautiful.'

It was. They passed orchards full of trees about to burst into blossom, and hedgerows bright with young growth. Soon they were among rolling fields where lambs, now nearly as big as their mothers, were grazing.

'Ah — the walls of stone. We have these too,' said Manolakis, pleased to find yet another bond with Britain. 'It is all so green.'

He appreciated the names of the villages they passed through, and made notes in his little book about the Swells and the Slaughters when they stopped for tea in a café where tulips and forget-me-nots were in full bloom in the garden.

'Shall we visit my sister now?' said Patrick, as he finished the last scone.

Liz looked taken aback.

'What an invasion for Jane,' she said.

Patrick's plans for the weekend had extended only as far as his visit to Pear Tree Cottage; he had given no thought to Saturday evening, nor to how they would spend Sunday. If he didn't know what to do at weekends, he usually visited Jane.

'Dimitris hasn't met her yet. It's a chance. She's used to me just turning up.'

'Yes — but three of us — suppose she's having a party?'

'We'll join in,' said Patrick blithely.

Dimitris did not understand why Liz was objecting. Greeks loved meeting one another.

'You do not like Patrick's sister?' he enquired.

'Of course I like her — I haven't seen her for ages, though. Anyway, I must think about getting back to London.'

'Why? You have someone to meet?' demanded Dimitris.

'No — no. Not this evening.'

'Liz, I thought you'd make a whole weekend of it,' Patrick said. 'Spend tonight in Oxford.'

Where, she wondered. Surely he did not mean at St Mark's?

'You haven't really got to get back?'

'I needn't, I suppose,' she said.

'Good, that's settled, then.'

'But I must leave tomorrow afternoon. I'm going to a concert in the evening,' Liz said firmly.

'Very well.'

With whom, Patrick wanted to know.

Jane, who was out in the garden cutting the withered blooms off daffodils, was surprised when a shabby Triumph Herald drew up outside the house, and at first she did not recognize Liz as she was helped to get out by a slight, dark man who sped round from the passenger's side to aid her. It was some seconds before the bulk of her brother extricated itself from the rear.

Liz hung back, shy now that they had arrived, but Manolakis was smiling eagerly, waiting to be introduced. Jane did her best to wear a welcoming expression; how like Patrick to turn up without even a telephone call; did they all expect to be fed? She shook hands with Manolakis, and told Liz how pleased she was to see her, which was true.

'Well, Patrick, what's happened to your passion waggon?' she enquired drily, and to Liz, 'Have you seen his new car?'

'Yes.' Liz began to laugh. 'Is that what you call it?'

'I do — the colour, and the room-for-two-only bit,' said Jane. 'It's his bird-catcher.'

'Jane, really—' Patrick looked cross and confused.

'Liz has known you for ever. I don't see why I have to censor my speech before her,' said Jane.

Manolakis was looking puzzled through this exchange.

'I do not understand, please,' he said.

'It's just as well,' said Patrick.

'I'll explain, Dimitri,' said Liz, who was still laughing.

'We've been to Stratford. There wasn't room for three of us in my car,' said Patrick sourly. 'Where's Michael?' At least he might expect some support from his brother-in-law.

'Fetching Andrew from a friend's house. He took Miranda with him,' said Jane. 'Come in. I'm sure you want a drink.'

She did not sound very hospitable, Patrick thought, as she led the way into the house. He turned to let Liz and Manolakis go ahead of him, but they were in a huddle, with Liz busy talking and Manolakis Listening intently, his hand on her arm; she must be explaining about the car.

'Have they been friends for long?' Jane asked, nodding towards the two.

'They met for the first time a few days ago. They get on very well, as you see,' said Patrick in an acid voice.

'Good,' said Jane. 'It's awkward when one's friends don't like each other.'

When Michael and the children returned, Manolakis was describing the Morris dancers and making a serious comparison between their performance and Greek dancing.

'The bells are—' he sought for the word.

'Quaint,' supplied Patrick.

'It's pretty energetic,' Jane said. 'Very good exercise for those taking part.'

'Bit folksy for me,' said Michael. 'Can't say I care for it.'

'Greek dancing's quite different,' Jane said. 'And so is the music — less jiggy — all that haunting melody. Bouzoukis aren't at all like concertinas.'

She went away to put the children to bed, and when she returned found that the three visitors were staying for supper, which Patrick had gone to buy at a Chinese takeaway place nearby. By the time he got back, more plans had been made.

'Dimitri's very keen to go to Woburn, and so's Liz,' Jane told him. 'So we're all going tomorrow. Liz is staying here for the night, but you and Dimitri will have to go back to Mark's — we haven't room for you all.'

Patrick gaped at Liz. What sort of betrayal was this? All the same, it did solve the problem of where she was to sleep, a matter to which he had not yet turned his mind.

'I thought you wanted to get back in good time tomorrow,' he said to her, nevertheless.

'I can go straight to London from Woburn,' said Liz.

'She's meeting her friend at the Festival Hall,' Jane informed him, spiking in a fresh barb. 'We must leave in good time — you must both get here promptly,' she added. 'We'll take a picnic.'

Patrick viewed the whole expedition with gloom. He was silent while they ate sweet and sour pork, chop suey and the various other dishes he had provided, but no one seemed to notice for they were all so busy talking themselves. At one point Jane asked Liz about the concert she was going to the next day, and learned that the London Symphony Orchestra, with Ivan Tamaroff, would be playing Mozart.

'Lovely. Wish I could come too,' said Jane.

'That is the man we saw at Stratford?' asked Manolakis.

'Yes.'

'I tried to get tickets for one of the concerts he's giving with his son — they're coming to Oxford,' said Jane. 'But they're sold out.'

Liz said she had two for their first London appearance.

Patrick was not knowledgeable enough about the music world to be familiar with more than the merest outlines of the Tamaroff story. Ivan, the father, had sought asylum in Britain eight years before when he came on a tour of Europe. His son was then still a student. The young man had never left Russia until two years ago, when he had played in Paris but without meeting his father. Now he was to be allowed to leave again.

'I hope they'll be able to play harmoniously together,' said Patrick.

'Why shouldn't they?' asked Jane.

'Two star performers.'

'You mean they might steal each other's thunder? Like actors sometimes do?' asked Liz. 'Surely not — they're father and son.'

Michael, listening to all this, thought that Patrick seemed to be in rather a bad mood. He decided it was time for a diversion, and switched the television on for the news. There was not much of interest on the political front, but there had been another art robbery in the Midlands. Porcelain, and a small painting by Corot, had been stolen from a house in Broadway.

'Broadway? We have been to this place today,' said Manolakis.

They had, but there had been no sign of police activity. The news report went on to add that the owner of the stolen articles had been at the theatre in Stratford-upon-Avon at the time of the robbery.

PART 12

I

St Mark's was impressive in the moonlight. The stonework, recently refaced, had a luminous look. Gargoyle faces stared down from the guttering as Patrick and Manolakis walked through the quadrangle to the staircase where Patrick had his rooms.

The two men paused to gaze at the pool in the centre of the quad, where fat carp lurked among lily leaves. The air around was fresh, and carried the scent of new-mown grass, for the gardeners had given the lawns their first cutting. Patrick loved the college at night, when it looked much as it had done for centuries.

'It is very good to spend your life in this place,' said Manolakis. 'And with young people — helping them to form wise thoughts — that is very good.'

Patrick thought that the most he could aspire to was opening their minds; any wise thoughts came in spite of him, and very often his pupils caused him to develop new opinions himself.

'But it is good to go to other places also,' said Manolakis, who was appreciating the effect of travel.

Patrick agreed.

'What is for the future? You will stay here always?'

'I don't know — maybe I'll look for a chair — apply for a senior post at another university eventually. But I don't know. I don't look very far ahead. What about you, Dimitri? Will you be Chief of Police in Heraklion one day? Or would you go to Athens?'

'I think I stay in Crete. Much happens there,' said Manolakis. 'It is good work. It is pleasant, too, for Ariadne and the children.' He had not thought of them for hours. 'And I make friends with the English visitors.'

Neither was tired. They sat in Patrick's sitting-room drinking whisky and talking. Each was content with his profession.

'If you had not been a teacher, Patrick, you should have been a policeman,' Manolakis said. 'Your friend Colin said that, too.'

Patrick could never imagine himself as a police inspector.

'Inspired guesswork is more my line,' he said. 'But I'm baffled about this business of Sam's. What do you make of it, Dimitri? It was you, after all, who sent me chasing this hare when you said I should find out about the body I'd seen. Should I go on, or do you think I should just forget it?'

'I think you must satisfy yourself, if it can be done. Otherwise you will be always wondering. Am I not right?'

He was.

'But if I can't find the answer?'

'Time will bring more events with him,' said Manolakis.

'It seems so extraordinary that Sam should have no real friends. No one really grieving. Very sad. And makes it difficult to learn about his life.'

To Dimitris it was dreadful.

'Yet he was your friend,' he said.

'You mean I should have known more about him? Seen him more?' It was easy to feel guilty now, when it was too late to change things. 'But we weren't really friends, Dimitri. Just acquaintances. He was in Austria — so was I — so was Liz. A man died, and we were all involved in the enquiries.' But

Sam kept apart from everyone else. He had never sought an audience — surely an unusual trait in an actor? Others Patrick had met enjoyed holding the floor off the stage, as well as on it. 'Your Greek directness — Anglo-Saxons do not have it in the same way,' he explained.

'It is a pity. It is your weather, perhaps,' said Manolakis.

'He should have gone to Greece — I know — that's what you're going to say,' said Patrick with a laugh.

'I am having an interesting holiday, Patrick, with this mystery with which you are concerning yourself,' said Manolakis earnestly.

What a complicated sentence, thought Patrick with admiration.

'Busman's holiday for you,' he said, and had to explain the saying.

Manolakis entered the phrase in his notebook.

'I thought perhaps you might have some professional excuse for your visit, yourself, Dimitri. Checking up on someone: something like that.'

Manolakis nodded.

'I have, perhaps, to go to Edinburgh. But we will see,' he said. 'It is a question of identity.'

II

Ten minutes before the appointed time the next morning, Patrick and Manolakis drove up to Jane and Michael's house in convoy, the Greek at the wheel of the MGB and Patrick in Liz's car, in which they had returned to Oxford. They were welcomed by Miranda, who was careering up and down the lawn pushing a small cart and chanting a strange song, while Andrew rode round on his bicycle uttering whooping cries.

The adults were in the kitchen, packing up the picnic. Patrick watched with approval as Michael loaded beer, orange squash and two bottles of wine into a basket.

'Can we help?' he asked.

'No. Just keep out of the way,' said Jane. 'Go away and read the papers.' She smiled kindly at Manolakis to show that she did not mean to seem harsh towards him.

Liz seemed remote, dressed in blue slacks and a paler blue shirt, and wearing a large apron printed with exotic fruit. Patrick hovered, wanting to be noticed, but she spared him no more than a glance as she sweepingly said 'hullo' to both him and Manolakis. He left Manolakis frowning over the *Sunday Times* and went out to clean the windscreen of her car. By the time she came out he had made a good job of the side and rear windows too, and was rubbing up the lights.

'I checked the oil and water this morning,' he told her. 'So she'll be all right for you to go back to London. She's done a big mileage this weekend.'

'Thanks.' Liz knew he would have filled up with petrol, too; after borrowing the car the day before to go to Pear Tree Cottage, he had returned it with a full tank. He was thoughtful and generous in so many ways, but he held back just when one expected, even hoped, that he might not. She had met plenty of men who were both material and emotional spongers, and Patrick was neither, so she smiled at him, and said again, 'Thanks very much, Patrick.'

Deciding how to travel took some time. Michael's Peugeot estate car would hold everyone, for the children were small, but Liz insisted on taking her car so that she could go straight on to London.

'You come with me, Dimitri,' she said, disposing of all argument. 'I'm sure you've had enough of Patrick for an hour or two.'

Manolakis climbed eagerly into the Herald, and as the small car drove off the others took their places in the Peugeot. Patrick sat in the back, with Miranda strapped into her seat on one side of him and Andrew on the other. All the way, the little boy kept watching for Liz's car and crying out 'There it is, no it isn't,' echoing Patrick's, thoughts. When at last they did pass the Herald, the two dark heads looked much too close together, and he was sure Manolakis had an arm along the back of Liz's seat.

But before they reached the game reserve, Patrick's conviction that the day would be a failure took a knock, for the approach was through acres of park-land where, in the spring sunlight, herds of deer could be seen grazing among the trees. So it must have looked, centuries ago.

Inside the safari park, however, he began to fret lest some lunatic beast set upon Liz's car; Manolakis, like all Greeks, would no doubt be valiant, but courage against a lion would not be enough. He was cheered at the sight of a warden in a zebra-striped Land Rover patrolling near the entrance.

'Animals shouldn't be taken out of their context,' he grumbled.

'But, Patrick, they're preserving them. They breed here,' said Jane.

'Jungle beasts belong in the jungle.'

'Look!' said Jane.

Huge animals, weird as creatures from another planet or another age, stood grouped in the sunlight ahead of them, their dull hides dun-coloured, their massive limbs looking as though they were built of armour-plating, not flesh and bone.

'Rhinoceroses!' Andrew cried.

The beasts were enormous. They looked peaceful, standing there. Ahead, Liz and Manolakis had stopped beside a pool in which two hippos were wallowing in the manner of the song.

Patrick's disapproval fell away, and he helped the children identify the other creatures they passed as they drove on. Andrew was intrigued by the electronic gates to the lion area; cars were admitted into a no-man's-land between two gates, the second, which let them into the section of the park where lions and tigers roamed, not opening until the first had closed behind them. A warden's cabin overlooked them both, and the whole area was securely fenced.

The first tiger they saw lay on a grassy bank under some trees; its coat shone sleekly, orange-coloured, with its black stripes gleaming.

'But it's splendid,' cried Patrick, in spite of himself. So far he had not seen a single monkey, although Andrew and Miranda kept pointing them out; he hated their all-knowing, human faces. He kept his eyes glued to the tigers. More could be seen, pacing slowly or lying about, impassive.

'Rhesus monkeys,' said Jane, and Patrick saw a little creature with a wrinkled old-woman face staring at him from a tree. He looked away, back at the tigers.

'They must be very well cared-for, here,' said Jane. 'They look so glossy, don't they?'

They did. The lions, by contrast, seemed drab, their colour dull and the males' manes looking unkempt, like tangled wool.

'Their ruffs should be made of silky hair,' said Jane. 'It's matted stuff, like sheep's wool.'

All agreed that the king of beasts looked less spectacular. Patrick was relieved when they emerged into the outer area, leaving the monkeys behind. Liz drove on in front, and after a while stopped so that they could get out and admire the elephants and the giraffes. Michael parked the Peugeot behind her car.

'Were they not fine animals?' Manolakis cried.

'Which did you like best, Dimitri?' Andrew asked him. 'I like the tigers. Grrr!' and he roared in imitation.

Patrick approached Liz.

'Well?' he said.

'You don't really like this sort of thing,' she said.

'You don't either — at least, you don't like circuses.'

She was surprised that he remembered this.

'You can't equate this with a circus. It's quite different, and today, with so few people about, it's rather splendid,' Liz said. 'But I wouldn't like to come when it's hot and crowded. We chose the best time.'

'Yes. I've quite enjoyed it, in fact,' said Patrick, and added, 'to my surprise.'

'You three go on to the house,' said Jane. 'We can't drag the children round it. We'll meet you near the entrance.'

They arranged a time, and Patrick clambered into the back of the Herald. He felt isolated, an outcast from the family group in the other car, and now playing gooseberry here. Gloomily, he stared out of the window as they drove past massed rhododendron bushes, not yet in bloom, towards the abbey.

'The first duke was a Roundhead. Did you know that, Patrick?' Liz remarked.

'A Roundhead? What is that, please?' asked Manolakis.

'He was against the king,' said Patrick.

'Oliver Cromwell served under him,' Liz said. 'Of course, he wasn't made a duke till much later.'

'We all have relations we're not too proud of,' said Patrick. 'How do you know all this?'

'It's in a book I found at Jane's,' Liz answered. 'The abbot of the day and two monks were hanged from an oak for speaking out against the marriage of Henry VIII and Anne Boleyn.'

'Do they haunt the place?'

'Not as far as I know — but there is supposed to be a ghost,' said Liz. 'I suppose there are in all these old houses.'

'If you believe in them,' said Patrick.

The abbey, as they approached, lay bathed in sunlight, a mellow building.

'It is like Oxford!' cried Manolakis.

Architecturally, it was. They went inside and were at once in the Grotto, an amazing apartment where the walls were covered in sea-shells like mosaics. The house was not crowded and they were able to move at their own pace. Liz particularly liked the porcelain, and Patrick the pictures.

'These old faces,' he said, standing on the staircase looking at a portrait of the third earl with his arm in a sling.

'They are like in the time of your Shakespeare,' said Manolakis, who was much taken with Lucy Harrington.

There was a minor commotion as they went through one long room, and the other sightseers separated to allow a small group through.

'VIPs,' said Liz. 'Look who's with them.'

Patrick recognized the tall young man who was personally guiding a party of three men through to the corridor beyond. It is not every day that a tourist sees a member of the peerage in the flesh, so this one had to be pointed out, and Manolakis duly observed the Marquess as he went past with his guests.

'Why, that's Senator Dawson with him,' said Liz. 'He was at Stratford. Remember, Dimitri?'

'You are right,' said Manolakis.

The senator was a slim man with grizzled hair cut neatly in the American style. He peered eagerly round through rimless spectacles as he walked along, hands clasped behind him, and nodded his thanks to the group of sightseers who had made way for his party. Patrick met his eye and thought how alert he looked; only later did he realize that there was a satisfied expression on his face, almost a look of triumph. Well, no doubt it was gratifying to come from the mid-West farm where he had been born to Washington, and eventually to visit this ancient place not like any humble tourist, but as an important guest.

'How were the Canalettos?' Jane asked, when they were reunited, and all sitting on rugs eating slabs of veal and ham pie under a huge oak tree.

'Overwhehning,' said Patrick. 'Almost too many at once.'

'It is very splendid in the house,' Manolakis said. 'You go there, Jane?'

'Another day,' said Jane. 'Let's wander round the stables — that's where the antique shops are, isn't it?'

The children were clamouring to go on the roundabout, so Michael took them off to the playground and the others strolled on through the courtyard towards the pottery and the shops. As they ambled along, they saw Senator Dawson again. His little group disappeared round a corner as they approached.

Patrick, who had been silent for some time, suddenly stopped.

'That's it!' he cried. 'Those pictures!'

'What pictures?' asked Jane.

'In the house — those old ones. Really old paintings are on wood — they're thick. Canvases are thinner.'

'What are you talking about?'

'Dendrochronology.'

'Whatever's that?'

'*Dendro* — it means a tree — and *chronos* is a year,' said Manolakis.

'Quite right,' said Patrick.

'Tree years?'

'Ring dating. The weather signatures.'

'Patrick, please, I do not understand,' said Manolakis.

'Ring dating — you mean that method of telling the dates of early paintings from the growth pattern on the wood they're painted on?' Liz asked.

'Exactly.' Patrick looked at her approvingly. He turned to Manolakis. 'There is a way of dating early paintings,' he explained. 'They were done on wood. The rings marking each year's growth follow a pattern according to the weather at the time. By recording the rings on various paintings it has been possible to date such paintings more accurately than before, and to prove which are the originals and which are copies.'

'Before cameras, much importance was for artists,' said Manolakis. 'It is what you see, and what I see, that may not be the same. But the camera — it tells the truth.'

Everyone listened respectfully to this remark. Then Liz brought them back to what had raised the subject.

'But why are you talking about this now, Patrick?'

'We were looking at those paintings in the house. It reminded me about the solidity of early portraits. Those awful paintings that girl Tessa had — they were solid. I'm wondering about them. The art robberies—' There had been several lately, all in the Midlands.

'You mean they could have been painted over, to hide what was really there?' Jane was used to what she thought of as Patrick's wild ideas and could follow his line of thought. 'But that would wreck them.'

'Not necessarily. Not if they were turned around and the backs painted. Or some sort of covering introduced,' said Patrick.

'Well!' Jane would have mocked the notion, but Patrick had been right about many strange things before. 'You mean that woman — Tina whatever-her-name-was — might have been mixed up with art thieves?'

'Perhaps without knowing it. She might have been looking after those paintings for a friend or something.' It sounded pretty unlikely, said aloud like this. 'I'd like to have another look at them.'

'Well, forget it now,' said Jane. 'Come on,' and she led the way into the nearest shop.

Michael and the children were looking at the monkeys in the playground area when they joined them later. Patrick glanced uneasily at the little beasts.

'Let's all go and have tea,' he said.

They sat in the sun outside a rotunda-style building with cardboard mugs of tea, fruit juice for the children, and a variety of cakes. Two peacocks prinked past, flirting their tails.

'Gorgeous, aren't they?' Liz said. The blue and green plumes shone in the sunlight; the birds' breasts were iridescent. 'What colours!'

'Their heads are strange,' said Manolakis. 'One — two bristles only.'

Everyone stared at the birds' heads, which were adorned by sparse feather coronets.

'They do look rather bald,' said Michael.

'These are not English birds,' Manolakis pronounced.

'They come from India and Ceylon,' said Patrick, pleased that he knew the answer. 'Pheasants of a sort, that's what they are.'

'They're almost too much of a good thing,' said Liz, who found herself unnerved by the calculating glare with which a nearby bird was eyeing her.

'Wouldn't you like to live in a stately home with peacocks on the lawn?' Michael asked her.

'No — not with mobs of people everywhere,' Liz said.

'But they are happy here, the people,' said Manolakis. 'Look at them.'

It was true. Everyone in sight looked thoroughly content.

'It is good to share this fine place with the people,' Manolakis went on.

'It's the only way they can make it pay,' said Patrick. He thought the modern, concrete pavilions which ministered to some of the wants of the visitors struck a crude note among the splendid background buildings, but how was such a problem of design to be solved? It was one which faced the university all the time. His eye lighted on a notice staked into the ground near them: *No Picnicing.*

'This illustrious family can't spell,' he said, and began to laugh.

'How very endearing,' Liz said.

Miranda had been tossing cake crumbs to the peacocks, and a handsome cock advanced towards her.

'I don't trust those birds,' said Jane. 'Keep away from it, Miranda.'

'Don't molest the bears,' said Liz dreamily.

'What?'

'It says that — or something like it — in Yellowstone Park,' said Liz. 'In America,' she added, to Manolakis.

'You have been there?' he asked, amazed.

'Yes.'

'And Patrick? Have you?'

'To New York,' he said. 'Never the west.'

Manolakis did not attempt to hide his envy.

'You'll have itchy feet now, Dimitri, after this trip of yours,' said Michael.

'Itchy feet! Ha!' Andrew liked this. 'Do they itch, Dimitri?'

'Like blazes,' said Manolakis, who had learned this phrase from Andrew earlier in the day.

Liz, who had felt herself suspended, all afternoon, in a limbo of contentment, decided that she must leave; the others, reluctantly, agreed that it was time for everyone to go. 'You have enjoyed yourself, Patrick, haven't you?' Liz asked him, as they walked back to the cars.

'Yes. But I still think lions and tigers belong in Africa, not Bedfordshire. Dartmoor ponies would look wrong in the veldt, don't you agree?'

'It's not a fair analogy,' Liz said.

'They'd be out of context,' Patrick insisted. 'Things aren't right, when they're misplaced.'

‘Like strawberries in November. They don’t taste as they should,’ Liz said.

‘And Brussels sprouts in June.’

‘I see what you mean, but I’m not sure I agree,’ she said. She turned to Jane. ‘Thank you for a lovely day, and for putting me up,’ she added.

Patrick and Manolakis, one on either side of her, shepherded Liz into her car. They both kissed her, then stood side by side waving her out sight.

‘Very salutary for Patrick, that,’ said Jane, watching.

‘He certainly does seem to be suffering,’ Michael admitted.

‘He takes her too much for granted — she’s handy, always there if he wants a companion for a night out in London. Do him good to realize she might not always be around,’ said Jane.

‘Why? Where might she go?’ demanded Andrew, who had been listening to this.

‘Oh — to Crete, to visit Dimitris,’ said Jane. ‘Now — into the car with you. We must go home.’

Patrick and Manolakis piled into the back of the Peugeot with the children.

‘I shall see Liz again tomorrow,’ Manolakis told them all. ‘I am going to London to visit her. We go to the theatre, and I take her to dinner. It will be very good.’

This news kept Patrick quiet all the way home.

PART 13

I

'You haven't seen a cross-section of British life,' Patrick told Manolakis over breakfast the next day. 'We must put that right.'

'You don't know what I have done when I have been in London,' said Manolakis, his large dark eyes glittering. 'Nor do you know what I shall do with Elizabeth. She will take me about. Her friends will be other.'

They would, but in what way? Patrick realized he had not met many of them and knew little of what she did between their meetings.

'Dimitri—' he said, and paused. He had no right to warn Manolakis off. What Liz did was her own affair, literally; he had no business to interfere.

'Yes?'

'Oh — nothing.'

How long did he mean to stay in London? More than one night? Patrick hoped not. Soon the college would be working at full stretch; the kitchen staff would be back on duty; Manolakis could be feasted off the college plate emblazoned with the winged lion of St Mark, and given the full treatment before he went home. He would like that. Or would he? Were there other things he might prefer?

'I have enjoyed it all so very much. It has been a privilege,' said Manolakis, looking earnestly at Patrick.

Patrick felt ashamed of his thoughts. He looked at *The Times* crossword to avoid the penetrating eye of the Greek.

'You might, perhaps, ask who made the identification of your friend Sam?' Manolakis suggested. 'There could be a way, through that person, to find out more of his life?'

Patrick sat up and threw down *The Times*.

'Good idea. Why didn't I think of it?' he exclaimed. 'But the police will have done it.'

'Yes, but you may have a new thought,' said Manolakis.

It was possible.

'I'll do as you suggest,' Patrick said. 'And I'll go back to Pear Tree Cottage for a look at those paintings. That will keep me busy while you're in London.'

He put Manolakis on the eleven forty-eight train to Paddington, and watched till he had vanished, giving an occasional restrained wave of the hand to acknowledge the Greek's less inhibited gestures from the window of his coach. Then he went back to St Mark's and rang up the *Evening Standard*. After that he set off for Stratford-upon-Avon, turning over in his mind what possible significance there could be in the fact that it was Leila Waters, the theatrical agent, who had officially identified Sam at the inquest, and that she had not told him this when they met.

Why should she? It was no secret. She probably thought that he knew.

II

Things were very different at Pear Tree Cottage. Curtains hung at the windows, there were tulips and lilac in vases, a line of washing, mostly faded, frayed jeans and drabhued singlets, hung between two apple trees in the garden.

Tessa, in a long cheesecloth dress with the arms of a maroon sweater protruding from its loose sleeves, was sitting at the kitchen table surrounded by piles of papers; they looked like bills.

'Hullo,' she greeted Patrick.

'I'm back rather soon,' he apologized. 'You've accomplished a lot over the weekend.'

'Yes — I'd plenty of help. I've got three lodgers now. They're all asleep,' she said. 'From the theatre — just walkers-on. So I'm financially solvent — or I thought I was.' She indicated the pile of papers. 'Tina's bills are following me.'

'You're not paying them, are you? You must pass them on to the executors,' said Patrick.

'Oh, I'm doing that all right. But I'm sorting them out. She owed for clothes, and electricity, and a man who did the garden at Strangeways has sent in a bill for twenty pounds. How do I know if he earned it?'

It would take months for things to be sorted out, Patrick knew; even a year. But better not depress her by saying so. She looked quite cheerful in spite of it all. He agreed that it would be difficult to check up on the gardener but thought he should probably have the benefit of the doubt.

'You've discovered no more about Sam Irwin?' he asked.

'Not a thing.'

'May I look at the theatre programmes again?'

'Of course. I found another great bundle of them.'

She settled him down with them, in a basket chair in the kitchen, and they sat there companionably, she totting up her aunt's debts and Patrick looking through the programmes. They went back over nearly twenty years and covered many celebrated productions.

'These might be quite valuable,' he said. 'Collections of almost anything are, you know.'

'I suppose they might be.'

'Don't throw them away without looking into it,' he advised.

'No, I won't.'

Many of the programmes included photographs of actors. Some were straight, without costume or make-up, but others showed them dressed for various roles and it was sometimes hard to recognize even well-known faces.

'She must have been really keen on the theatre to keep all these,' said Patrick.

He supposed that if the names on the programmes were fed into a computer, a pattern might show whose appeared most, possibly indicating any she followed particularly; but such an exercise might only prove that Tina had seen many of the great performances in recent years, as he had himself.

'Did she know Joss Ruxton?' he asked.

'I've no idea. Couldn't you ask him?' said Tessa.

'I expect so.' Patrick got up. 'Those pictures — have you hung them anywhere?'

'I've got rid of them,' said Tessa. 'Isn't it marvellous? I sold the lot for sixty pounds — wasn't it a fantastic price to get for them? It'll buy a mower for all this wild grass.' She waved a hand in the direction of the open back door.

Patrick was taken aback at this.

'Who bought them?' he asked.

'Some man called Gulliver — he's got a gallery in Stratford. He came round touting. Yesterday morning, it was. He said the tourists would grab them. Fancy coming on Sunday,' she marvelled.

Fancy indeed, thought Patrick, his suspicions growing.

'I might have got more, by haggling a bit, but a bird in the hand, and all that, I thought,' Tessa was saying.

'Quite,' said Patrick. There was no more to be learned here, it seemed. 'I'll be off, then,' he added. He must find Gulliver quickly.

''Bye. Thanks for calling,' said Tessa.

He left her still frowning over her aunt's bills and as he made his way out through the front of the house, he encountered a youth at the foot of the staircase. He was short, pale, and had shoulder-length hair and a large moustache. Patrick knew that he must be a spear-carrier or a tribune.

'Hi,' said the youth as they passed.

'Hi,' said Patrick, feeling huge and healthy by contrast. He walked on.

'Darling, I'll die if I don't have some coffee,' he heard the youth say, and Tessa made some soothing response.

He went on down the path and got into his car. There, he opened the glove compartment and put into it two theatre programmes which, without Tessa seeing, he had filched from her pile. They contained photographs which he wished to study at leisure.

III

The gallery Tessa had mentioned was in a narrow alley behind a solidly restored brick building through whose leaded window panes Patrick could discern folk-weave caftans and peasant blouses hanging from the beams amid festoons of costume jewellery.

A sign beside the building pointed the way to Gulliver's Gallery, and Patrick followed it along a cobbled path to a barn set in a yard behind the boutique. The walls inside the gallery were hung with new masters, and Gulliver himself, a small man with a pointed beard modelled on that of Shakespeare, stood at an easel in a corner busily turning out another. Scenes of Stratford-upon-Avon were ranged along one wall, facilely executed and easy on the eye, but commonplace. On another wall hung copies of Victorian illustrations to the plays, darkly painted and sombre: Macbeth loomed through thick Scottish mist, and the body of Ophelia drifted, flower-bedecked, in a river that seemed to flow through an underground cavern. Patrick could see nothing remotely like any of the paintings that had been at the cottage. If they were disguised stolen ones, perhaps they had already been passed on.

'Can I help you?' asked Gulliver, when he had prowled around for some time and finally come to rest in front of

Shylock, knife raised, towering over a bare-chested, fainting Antonio with madly rolling eyes.

Patrick, the only customer in the gallery, put on his most urbane expression.

'Do you do these yourself?' he asked.

'Most of them, yes,' said Gulliver. 'I can turn out Anne Hathaway's cottage in less than an hour.'

Patrick inspected the work on his easel. It showed the young Shakespeare poaching at Charlecote.

'They go quite fast when the season proper begins,' said Gulliver. 'It's only just starting, you know.'

As if on cue, there came the sound of footsteps on the cobbles outside and the chirrup of feminine voices. In came a posse of some twenty or more American matrons; they flowed around the aisles and Patrick was swamped. Sure enough, they were eager purchasers, and soon Gulliver was busy exchanging his wares for travellers' cheques. He wrapped the pictures in brown paper, fastening the corners with sticky tape. Patrick watched in fascination. Every tourist bought something — if not a painting, then a pottery medallion or a plaster bust of Shakespeare. Reinforcements arrived, in the shape of a female whom Patrick silently christened, however implausibly, Stella, to help with the parcelling. She was fifty-ish and plump, and wore a homespun dress, thereby adding to the cottage-industry atmosphere. Further copies of the church, and Clopton Bridge by moonlight, were obtained from the rear of the shop; there seemed to be an unending supply. Doubtless Gulliver spent the winter in his *atelier,* turning them out.

A blue-rinsed woman with the petite wrists and ankles common to so many Americans was enquiring for a picture of Othello suffocating Desdemona. Her schedule had not allowed her time to see the play, she said, so she wanted to take back a picture instead.

To fetch Othello, Stella had to visit her store behind the scenes; however, she reappeared quickly with the desired picture, ready wrapped. Patrick, ostensibly studying Lear depicted with leaves in his hair and wearing a goatskin, watched from the corner of his eye as the American woman shelled out dollars. The party, in twos and threes, began to drift off, declaring that their coach would be waiting. They were due at Shottery next.

Patrick, his eye taken by Miranda playing chess with Ferdinand, thought it would be an appropriate purchase because of the family link, so he bought it; when it had been wrapped he ambled out of the studio in the wake of the Americans.

They were piling out of their coach in the car-park when he arrived at Shottery soon afterwards. He watched them go up the road towards Anne Hathaway's cottage; they carried their purses, but not their recent purchases, which were left in the coach. Patrick saw the driver lock the door.

The group would not be gone long, Patrick knew, for they must be due elsewhere — at Warwick Castle, perhaps, and to Blenheim for tea. He waited. Less than half an hour later they filtered back; heads were counted; they took their seats, and were off.

He followed them all the afternoon, until the coach finally stopped at a hotel near the West London Air Terminal where they were booked in for the night. Baggage was hauled from the luggage compartment and piled with handbags and carriers in the busy foyer as keys and rooms were allocated, and registrations made.

Patrick watched while the Othello painting was laid down on a leather seat beside a navy jersey coat and a clutch of tourist literature. There was room for him on the seat too, and he sat there reading the *Evening Standard* which he had bought from the kerbside vendor outside the hotel while he watched the coach disgorge. When he got up and sauntered out a few minutes later, Miranda and Ferdinand, indistinguishable in their brown paper wrappings from the picture of Othello, had taken his place, and Patrick bore off with him towards Oxford the image of the Moor.

PART 14

I

The picture had been clamped into a mock-old plastic-moulded, gilt-painted frame. It lay on the table between Patrick and Humphrey Wilberforce. Othello, bow-legged, his toga rent, glowered at the shrinking Desdemona whose opulent bosom threatened to escape from her chiton-like nightdress.

'Terrible, isn't it?' said Patrick cheerfully.

'And this fellow charges twenty-five pounds a time, you say?'

'Yes.'

'Well—' Words failed Humphrey. 'What has this to do with me?' he asked.

'I want you to prise it apart. I daren't touch it — I might wreck it.'

Humphrey's expression indicated that this would be a service to art.

'Whatever for? Are you collecting plastic frames?' he enquired.

'I think there may be something underneath Othello.'

Humphrey made a crude remark.

'I mean,' said Patrick patiently, 'I think it may cover some other painting. A stolen one.'

'Pretty small,' said Humphrey.

'A little Corot,' Patrick suggested.

Humphrey cast him a sharp look.

'That robbery — no, Patrick. How could it?'

'I may be entirely wrong — I rather hope I am — but I don't want to go wasting people's time at Scotland Yard or the National Gallery if that's the case.'

'And my time's expendable,' said Humphrey.

'If I'm right, we pass it on at once. If not, there's no harm done.'

'Hm.' Humphrey picked the picture up, balancing it between his hands. 'It is a bit heavy for what it seems to be,' he said. 'I suppose we'd better proceed with infinite caution. Come along.'

Patrick followed him into his studio, where very gingerly Humphrey, who was primarily a historian but also a painter in his spare time, carefully damped the edges of the paper backing on the mount. They waited in silence until it began to curl, and then Humphrey began to ease it off. Behind it was a layer of thicker paper.

'This is rather odd,' said Humphrey, now intrigued. He took a tiny knife out of a drawer and inserted it under the edge of the frame; the plaster cracked at once. 'Not at all strong,' he said. 'I suppose they were trying to keep the weight down.'

'So there is something there?'

Humphrey worked very slowly and carefully now, easing the frame off the canvas it surrounded. The paper that covered the back of the painting extended over the front edges, and the canvas bearing the representation of Othello was attached to it by some sort of strong glue. Humphrey separated the paper at the side and tore away a tiny part of it. Under it could be seen a fragment of canvas much older, and covered in darker paint.

'I'd better stop,' he said reluctantly. 'I'm not an expert on stolen property, and I may obscure clues if I go on. There's another picture here. The monstrosity is stretched over the back of it, I think.' He looked longingly at the thick paper.

'It's probably got some other layer beneath, as protection, but they'll have wanted it to be ventilated in some way. I don't suppose it was intended to be left like this for long.'

Patrick thought of the American lady, no doubt due to board a plane the next day. She would not discover the substitution until she reached home. It would not be difficult to trace her, but Gulliver himself was the person the police would want to question. He wondered how best to tackle the next step; a special department at Scotland Yard dealt with art thefts, though doubtless the local police did on-the-spot investigations. Colin would know whom to approach. Meanwhile there was the question of the picture's safety.

'You get on to some of your police chums,' said Humphrey, whose thoughts had meanwhile run parallel. 'I'll keep the painting safe for the moment. I'm sure it'll be taken off my hands very swiftly. How on earth did you stumble on this racket, Patrick?'

'Quite by chance — because of a poodle,' said Patrick.

'I don't see the connection.'

'Nor do I, yet, but there must be one.'

If, in fact, other missing masterpieces were hidden under the dark paintings he had seen at Pear Tree Cottage, was Tina keeping them for Gulliver to collect?

'What made you suspect there was something wrong about this picture?' Humphrey asked.

'I thought it strange that a woman should want a painting of this particular moment in the play and carry it away without looking at it. The parcel was brought to her ready wrapped, from the rear of the gallery.'

'I see. It was a bit of luck you happened to be there at the time.'

'Yes, it was. But it wasn't the only picture being smuggled out like that. If I'm right, there's a constant stream of them. There have been several art thefts in the Midlands lately and I think Gulliver has a good racket going — painting them over and passing them on. And maybe passing on the proceeds of other people's thieving too.' For if the pictures he had taken from Tessa were also disguised masterpieces, someone else had already blotted them out: unless Gulliver had been using the empty cottage as a hiding-place, in which case Tina wasn't involved.

But the pictures had come up with all her furniture. Or had they?

II

He put this theory to Detective Inspector Colin Smithers on the telephone.

'If the cottage was a hiding-place, and if Sam was going there, for whatever reason,' he said, thinking of the Earl Grey tea, 'he might have stumbled on what was going on.'

There were sacks in the garage of Pear Tree Cottage, and fragments of sacking had been found under Sam's fingernails. But if he was trussed up at Pear Tree Cottage, why dump him in the Thames when the Avon was close by?

'Have your colleagues got a lead on Sam?' he asked.

'Not as far as I know,' said Colin. 'You know how much of our work is dogged routine checking, Patrick.'

'I had an idea about him,' Patrick said. 'But it's so unlikely that I won't mention it yet.'

'Look for some evidence,' Colin advised. 'Meanwhile, I'll send our art boys up to get your picture. We don't want that trail to get cold.'

'I doubt if Gulliver's in it alone,' said Patrick. 'He's the receiver and the despatcher. Others do the thieving, I surmise.'

'Probably. I expect they'll set some sort of trap to catch the lot of them,' said Colin.

'Have you seen Dimitris?' Patrick asked. 'He's back in London now.'

'I know. The business he came over about has just finished,' said Colin. 'His nephew died of drugs some time ago, over here. Dimitri came over for the hearing. He was in court today. He didn't tell you, did he?'

'No. How dreadful.'

'He wanted to see justice done, and repent back to the family.'

'I see.'

Patrick was sorry for what had happened, but obscurely elated because Manolakis had not gone to London solely to see Liz.

PART 15

I

Leila Waters looked across her desk at Patrick. A faint smell of hot cheese from the pizzeria below wafted into the office through the fractionally opened window.

'Yes. I identified Sam,' she said.

'But why you? Wasn't there a relative?'

'We knew of no one. It was either me or someone from the company. I probably knew him as well as anyone.'

'Yet you didn't know much about his private life.'

'No one did,' said Leila. 'The police were quite satisfied for me to do it — I'd known him for years.'

'Wasn't it rather a distressing experience?'

'What do you think? Do you know what the water does to people?'

Patrick knew a lot about drowned bodies. Sam's was not the only one he had seen.

'He'd dyed his hair for Macduff?'

'Yes — he preferred it to wearing a wig.'

'But he didn't grow a beard?'

'No — he'd have had to dye that too, wouldn't he? And that wouldn't have been so easy,' said Leila.

'But he did wear a beard for Macduff?'

'Yes.'

'He was good at make-up, wasn't he? He's unrecognizable in some of his old photographs.' Patrick leaned across the desk and handed her one of the theatre programmes appropriated from Tessa. It showed a fat, elderly man: Sam, padded in face and body, playing Falstaff.

'True enough. Make-up does wonders. But that was gross miscasting,' Leila said. 'Sam wasn't a good Falstaff.'

'Why? Too much unlike his own personality?'

'Yes.'

'Surely that's the test of an actor — to go against type?'

'Up to a point.'

'It's easier to act a role like your own nature?'

'Not necessarily. Sometimes it can be a release to play another sort of person.' She tapped the programme. 'It was a long time ago — before he lost his nerve.'

'You had no doubts about his identity when you saw the body?'

'No. Nor did the woman who recognized him when he was dragged out of the river. She knew him at once.'

'Who was she?' asked Patrick.

'I don't know her name. Some passer-by.'

'Was she at the inquest?'

'No. It wasn't necessary — it was just a preliminary enquiry so that the funeral could take place. Perhaps she'll be at the resumed inquest,' said Leila. 'Now, I really am very busy.'

Patrick departed; he was the object of interested scrutiny from the patient clients lined up in the outer office, and this time the receptionist even gave him a smile.

II

Sergeant Bruce was writing a report when Patrick was shown into the busy office where he occupied a corner.

'Ah — good morning, sir,' he greeted Patrick.

'Good morning, sergeant. You remember we met at Sam Irwin's flat?'

'I do, sir.'

'You asked me to let you know if I thought of anything pertinent to your enquiries.'

'That's right, sir. And you have, I take it.'

'I wondered how you got on to Miss Waters. The theatrical agent. How you came to suggest that she should identify the body.'

'They told us at the theatre. No one there was keen to do it. Seems they think that play's an unlucky one.'

'Oh.' Now he mentioned it, Patrick seemed to remember hearing about some theatrical superstition concerned with *Macbeth*. 'So you went to see her. What about the woman who recognized the body at the time it was found?'

'Just a bystander. Knew him right away, but not in a position to give official recognition, legally speaking.'

'I see. Who was she, sergeant?'

Sergeant Bruce looked at him, then made up his mind.

'You were there, after all. Might have overheard her telling me, if you'd lingered on the spot,' he said. 'She was Mrs Amy Foster — from Putney. A hundred and eighty-seven, Montagu Court, that's it — it's a big modem block of flats up on the hill,' the sergeant told him, referring to a note.

'Keen theatregoer, eh?'

'Yes, sir, so it seems. Quite a fan.'

'Hm. Thanks.'

'What's on your mind, sir?'

'I'm not sure. It might be worth while, though, sergeant, looking through the pathologist's report. Or if it's not mentioned, asking him.'

'Asking him what?'

'About the beard of the deceased. What colour it was. It goes on growing, doesn't it, after death?'

III

Patrick drove straight to Putney, over the bridge and up the hill, where there were several blocks of flats, he knew. He pulled into a side road and soon found a postman who directed him to Montagu Court. It was a large, new block, and there was a porter.

'Mrs Amy Foster?' The porter shook his head. 'We've no Mrs Amy Foster here. Of course, she could be staying with someone. But there's not been any mail for her.'

'A hundred and eighty-seven, that's the number,' Patrick repeated.

'Well now, sir, you are asking for something. You must have come to the wrong block.'

'It's the address I was given,' said Patrick.

'There's no such number here,' said the porter. 'We stop at a hundred and sixty. I'm afraid Mrs Amy Foster's been pulling your leg, sir.'

It took Patrick a second or two to realize that the porter thought Mrs Amy Foster must be someone who did not wish to encourage his pursuit of her.

'Why not invent the name of the block, then, as well as the number?' he snapped.

‘Why not, sir, as you say. Perhaps she didn’t want to tell too big a fib. You might know Putney quite well, eh?’

The porter could be right, for the police must know the various blocks of flats. The lady might not want to be traced for all manner of reasons. Perhaps she was not supposed to be in London at the time. Perhaps she was not Mrs Amy Foster at all.

PART 16

I

It would be pleasant to spend the evening with Liz and Manolakis, Patrick decided, driving slowly back towards the river. Perhaps the Greek would be ready to return with him to Oxford that evening.

He found a telephone box, stopped, and rang up Liz. She sounded in a hurry, and said that they were just off to a concert.

'But Dimitri isn't musical,' said Patrick.

'How do you know?' asked Liz. 'He's not had much chance to find out, in fact. I've got these tickets, and he wants to go.'

She seemed to spend her whole time going to concerts, Patrick thought crossly.

'Is everything all right?' he asked.

'Of course,' she answered. 'Why shouldn't it be?'

This conversation left him very bad-tempered, and the rush-hour traffic, in which he soon found himself wedged, did not help. He might as well go back to Oxford, he thought, for he had reached a dead-end here, and by now Humphrey might have news about the picture which could lead to something else.

Sam had possessed sodium amytal tablets. Tina Willoughby had swallowed barbiturates. Neither had left suicide notes. Both appeared to have plans for the future. Tina had probably been having an affair with Hugo Barry her neighbour; the ending of that, if it was over, might have disturbed her, but Hugo's wife thought she had an actor friend. Sam was an actor, but did not show much interest in women. Pictures of dubious origin had been among Tina's possessions and had been swiftly wafted away. Earl Grey tea had been in her house and also in Sam's flat. Those were the known facts.

Tessa might know how long her aunt had owned those paintings. He could go and ask her.

Always more cheerful when he had thought of some positive action, Patrick pressed on through the traffic. He would call at Jane's on the way home; she'd be eager to hear the latest developments, he was sure.

He arrived just as she and Michael were starting dinner.

'Lucky it's not chops,' she said. 'We can spare you some shepherd's pie.'

While they ate, he told them how puzzled he was.

'You still don't know that Sam and Tina were acquainted, do you?' Jane enquired.

'No.'

'Do you think this Hugo fellow was having an affair with Tina, and then she dropped him for Sam, and so he pushed Sam in the river?' Jane asked. 'It's a bit unlikely, isn't it?'

'When you say it like that, yes,' said Patrick. 'But these things do happen. I'm not surprised if Hugo Barry was having an affair with her. His wife seems a very tough nut — and she's got that awful little dog.'

'If she's got a philandering husband that's why, I expect,' said Jane tartly.

'He seemed an amiable sort of man,' said Patrick.

'Maybe he beat her. Or indulged in horrid practices,' said Jane.

'How gruesomely your mind works, darling,' said Michael. 'No one would think it to look at you. It must run in the family.'

'I wonder what Tina looked like,' Patrick said. 'It might help to see a photograph of her.'

'What difference does it make?' asked Michael.

'Well — you can make an assessment of someone when you know what they're like in appearance,' Patrick said.

'The niece would have a photograph, wouldn't she?' Jane suggested.

'I suppose she might,' said Patrick, brightening. To ask her for one would give him an excuse to find out more about the pictures.

'I'm surprised you didn't think of that yourself,' said Jane drily. 'But really, Patrick, I think you're exaggerating all this. It's just two tragic suicides, with no connection.'

'Maybe,' said Patrick. 'But what I'm not exaggerating is finding a stolen picture.'

He told them about Gulliver's Gallery and what had led him there.

Jane and Michael listened in silence.

'Well,' said Michael at the end of the account, 'I must hand it to you. You certainly get results. I wouldn't like to have some skeleton in my cupboard I wanted to keep from you. You do have an uncanny instinct.'

'If I do, then that's what's telling me there's something suspicious about poor Sam's death, and Tina's too,' said Patrick.

'You think Tina's tasteless paintings were cover-ups too, do you?' Jane asked.

'I do. Some Tudor portraits were taken a few weeks ago from near Birmingham — do you remember that? There have been a lot of art robberies lately — there must be quite a gang at work. Gulliver may be just the camouflager and middleman.'

'It's all so complicated,' Jane complained.

'Yes, it is. But it's like teasing a splinter out of your finger — you worry away at it, thinking it's small, and suddenly up comes a great spike,' said Patrick. 'There's only one thing certain, and that is that Tessa Frayne, the niece, is not mixed up in anything, even if her aunt was. She'd never have told me about Gulliver's Gallery, if she was.'

'I'm surprised he told her who he was, if he's a crook,' said Michael.

'His business is authentic enough. The more straightforward his manner, the less he had to fear from her,' said Patrick. 'He must have passed those pictures on promptly. They were too big for a tourist to carry out — he may have other outlets.'

'Could Sam have been an art thief?' Jane said. 'Perhaps he thought he'd been discovered and killed himself before he was arrested.'

'I can't see Sam as a villain, somehow,' Patrick said. 'He was more the victim type.'

'Could he have got carried away by some part he was playing? If he had to act an evil role every night, it might have become a habit.'

'I doubt it — not unless he was schizoid. But he was playing Macduff, and he's not a villain,' said Patrick.

'Well, the police will be chasing up this picture, won't they?' Michael said. 'They'll soon get to the bottom of it. If Sam was mixed up with the art thieves, they'll find out and that will give them a line on his death.'

Patrick supposed that this was fair reasoning.

When they had finished their meal, the two men went into the sitting-room while Jane made coffee. Patrick sank down on the large, sagging sofa, and Michael put on the television news. The main item was a kidnapping in America; they saw distraught relatives and shots of FBI men with guns. Looking relieved at having a pleasant item to relate, the announcer then declared that Sasha Tamaroff, the son of the pianist Ivan, had arrived in London for his concert tour and for his first meeting with his father for many years. They were to perform together at the Queen Elizabeth Hall the following week and give other concerts in different parts of the country. There was film of the violinist's Aeroflot plane arriving at Heathrow and of father and son embracing. Then they were shown driving away in a large limousine.

'We saw him at Stratford — the father,' Patrick said. 'In the audience for *Othello*. Must be rather poignant for them. I hope they like one another.'

'I'm rather surprised they've let Sasha come,' said Michael. 'Do you think he'll go back?'

'Maybe he's left a wife or someone behind as a hostage,' said Patrick.

'Ivan Tamaroff was to have played at the Festival Hall tonight,' the announcer was continuing. 'But unfortunately he injured his hand recently and is unable to play. He is confident the injury will clear up in time for his first appearance with his son.' And he went on to explain that another well-known pianist had taken his place as the solo player with the London Symphony Orchestra. Father and son were in the audience instead. Shots followed of the two entering the Festival Hall, smiling broadly, the father white-haired, with strongly marked brows above dark eyes, and the son slighter, looking very youthful. Ivan Tamaroff's hand was tucked into a narrow sling and rested on his chest.

'Wonder what you'd look like wearing a white wig and bushy eyebrows, Mike,' Patrick mused.

'Rather old, I should think,' said Michael. 'What an odd speculation.'

'Mm. I just thought Ivan looked a bit like an actor I once saw made up as Gloucester, in *Lear*,' said Patrick. 'It's amazing how they can alter their faces.'

'Yes, false noses and things. But what are you getting at?'

'I'm not quite sure,' said Patrick. 'But I'm thinking of something that Dimitris said. It's a question of identity.'

PART 17

I

The picture concealed under Othello was the missing Corot. It was quite undamaged; the new painting had been done on a fine canvas stretched across the back of the original. Humphrey Wilberforce was very excited about it.

It was the next morning; he and Patrick' were both in Humphrey's rooms, talking to Detective Chief Inspector Frobisher who was investigating the Midlands art robberies. The police would descend on Tessa now and upset her: it was unfortunate, Patrick felt, but could not be helped.

But the chief inspector had different ideas.

'Please keep very quiet about this, Dr Grant,' he said. 'We need to get whoever's behind it all. This Gulliver may be just a link in the chain. And the late Mrs Willoughby another, very likely.'

Patrick saw a ray of light.

'So you won't be seeing Miss Frayne?'

'Not at once, though we shall need to eventually.'

'I could do it for you,' Patrick suggested. 'I could lead the conversation around to her aunt. And look about for more pictures at the same time, perhaps.' Since he meant to do it anyway, he might as well acquire official blessing.

The chief inspector had heard something of Patrick's reputation by now, but had not yet decided if it was an advantage or not.

'Well, yes,' he said slowly. 'Perhaps that would be an idea.'

'What do you particularly want to know?' Patrick asked. 'I could go to Stratford today.'

'Anything at all that you can manage to find out. Perhaps Dr Wilberforce would go with you,' suggested Frobisher. 'His knowledge of art might be useful. Or one of our trained officers, in plain clothes.'

Patrick thought that a plain clothes officer, even if he did not look like a policeman, would give out an aura.

'How about it, Humphrey?' he asked. 'It seems a good thought.'

Humphrey could scarcely wait to be off.

They departed after lunch, in Patrick's car.

'What are we going to do?' Humphrey asked. 'How shall we tackle this assignment?'

'We'll improvise,' said Patrick. 'We'll ask Tessa how long her aunt had had those paintings, and if she knows where they came from, but we'll wrap it up subtly so that she barely notices.'

When they reached the cottage, Tessa was not to be seen. The young man whom Patrick had met before was in the garden in the spring sunshine, in a semi-kneeling position, sitting on his heels on a rug on the lawn. His hands were clasped behind his back and he gazed at the sky, seeming unaware of their approach.

'Meditating,' said Patrick calmly, and stepped heavily on the flagged path so that his footfalls were loud.

The young man took no notice.

'Hullo! Is Tessa about?' Patrick cried heartily.

The young man blinked, then focused on them.

'No — sorry — she's shopping. She won't be long. Go in and wait for her, won't you?' he said.

'Right, we will. Don't let us disturb you,' said Patrick.

The young man needed no such instruction; he bent forward and touched his head to the ground in front of his knees, remaining there, motionless, Patrick gave Humphrey a meaningful look and hurried on into the cottage.

'We can have a look round,' he said when they were inside. 'Before she gets back, I mean. The guru will be oblivious for hours.'

'They say it's good for the nerves,' remarked Humphrey.

But Patrick had no time to discuss yoga techniques now.

'I'm nipping out to look at something in the garage,' he said. 'Give a shout if Tessa comes back. And watch out generally, Humphrey. There are others here — she's got more than one lodger.'

He went through to the kitchen, opened the back door and strode rapidly over the lawn to the garage. The sacks which he had seen on his earlier visit had disappeared.

'That was quick,' said Humphrey when he reappeared. 'What were you looking for?'

'Tell you later,' replied Patrick.

He moved round the sitting-room, which was rather untidy, peering at the objects scattered about. There were papers heaped on several chairs, and a marked copy of *Henry V* lay open, face downwards, on an arm of the sofa.

Patrick picked it up and saw, riffling the pages, that the part of the boy was underscored.

'Looks as if someone here's got a few lines to say after all,' he said.

Humphrey was looking at the porcelain. He picked up one or two objects that were on a window sill and inspected them.

'Pretty, but not of any great value,' he said, and began prowling round looking at the paintings. There were some landscapes, one with a windmill by a stream, the other of a tree bent in a gale; they were starkly done, quite compelling, obviously modern.

'Harmless,' he pronounced.

'No hidden masterpieces?'

'Not at first glance.' Humphrey tapped the paintings with a fingernail, then lifted them away from the wall. 'No, they're just what they seem to be,' he said.

Patrick had been diverted by the bookcase, where he found a row of modern novels in paperback, some poetry, and various classic authors including Hardy and Jane Austen.

'Tessa reads,' he said. 'That's good.'

'Might be the deceased aunt,' Humphrey answered, coming to examine the collection.

They looked inquisitively inside various volumes but found no names inscribed. Both were sitting quietly reading when the blond young man reappeared from the garden, Humphrey with a book of verse in his hand, and Patrick absorbed by wartime Athens in Olivia Manning's *Friends and Heroes*. They glanced up, smiled benevolently at him, and resumed their reading.

The youth crossed the room, picked up the marked copy of *Henry V*, and turned its pages.

'Would one of you mind giving me my cues?' he asked.

'What? Oh, hear your lines, you mean? Yes, certainly,' said Patrick.

'I'd like to run through them,' said the youth, looking severe. 'I'm understudying the boy, in *Henry V*.'

'Oh — splendid! I'd like to say I hope you get the chance to perform, but that would be hard luck on the principal,' said Patrick.

'Well — you never know. He's understudying the Dauphin. We might all change round,' said the young actor hopefully.

'Come on, then.' Patrick was eager to help. 'Give me the book,' and he began, before he had the right page open, '"Oh hound of Crete, think'st thou my spouse to get?"' and went on to the end of the speech before the boy's entrance without once glancing at the text.

The actor's jaw had dropped; even Humphrey was impressed.

'Come on, come on,' said Patrick. '"Mine host Pistol—" on you go.'

'You know it,' said the actor.

'Of course I know it,' said Patrick testily.

Humphrey began to titter.

'You two can never have been properly introduced,' he said.

'You're not in the business, are you?' asked the young man in accusing tones.

'I lecture about Shakespeare at Oxford,' said Patrick. 'Now, come along.'

When Tessa returned some time later, she could hear them before she entered the cottage. One voice, somewhat declamatory, which she had heard speaking the part before, described the flea upon Bardolph's nose; a deeper, firm voice replied, and doubled for the part of Nym, while Pistol spoke in rather unnatural tones and stumbled over the bit about oaths being straws and faiths wafer cakes, a real tongue-twister, as she knew. She listened outside for a minute, and then came in as the scene ended. The paid-up member of Equity stood on the hearth-rug, looking dramatic, while beside him was Patrick Grant, hair flopping over his brow, hazel eyes shining behind his spectacles. An unknown man, looking rather frail, with a high domed forehead and slightly receding sandy hair, held open a book and declared as she entered: '"Let housewifery appear: keep close, I thee command."'

II

Tessa stood on the threshold of the room, shaking with laughter.

'Right on cue,' she said.

Humphrey and Patrick both shared her mirth, but the genuine actor looked outraged.

'There's a rehearsal tomorrow. I must be ready,' he said.

'Of course you must, Adrian. And you are,' said Tessa. 'Let's all have tea. I'll put the kettle on while you run through it again.'

The two visitors had not explained their presence, but she seemed to need no reason. She was accustomed, Patrick realized, to men coming to see her just because they wanted to. With rather more self-consciousness this time, he and Humphrey flung themselves into their roles again. Adrian wanted to go on to the battle scene, but Tessa reprieved them by calling from the kitchen that tea was ready.

Adrian did not know whether he approved of Patrick; his familiarity with the text was awesome, and he read — or rather, spoke — it well, but the unaffectedness of his manner might be deceptive; he could be secretly mocking. Sulking somewhat, he said he would go upstairs.

'What — no tea?' Patrick asked.

'Come on, Adrian. There's apricot jam,' called Tessa. 'You'd better have something — you missed lunch.'

'Oh — if you insist.'

With scant grace, Adrian followed the others into the kitchen where among the cups and saucers on the table was a fresh, crusty loaf, half a pound of butter on a blue plate, and a new pot of jam.

Humphrey's eyes brightened.

'What a splendid sight,' he said, rubbing his hands. 'Patrick, you haven't introduced me.'

He beamed at Tessa, and she smiled back.

'Humphrey Wilberforce,' he said, bowing from the waist.

'Hullo, Humphrey. Have a seat,' said Tessa, waving at the stools which stood around the large table.

Patrick warmed to her; what a nice, natural girl. Then he glanced at Humphrey and saw his own feelings reflected in his colleague's thin, rather careworn face. Humphrey, a shy man in women's company, was smiling and relaxed, watching Tessa pour tea into blue cups. Adrian was told to cut the bread. Soon all were eating thick, crookedly cut slices, rather greedily spread; they were soft and doughy, and utterly delicious. Patrick, between mouthfuls, held forth at some length about the tensions there must be for an understudy who, however much he might hope to be called on, would feel fright on the night.

'Adrian's just longing for the chance, aren't you?' said Tessa. 'You'll get some real parts at the end of the season, I'm sure.'

'You're good as the boy. It's an important part,' said Patrick.

Adrian unbent at this praise, and told them about the importance of movement, getting up to demonstrate.

'Are you both Shakespearian scholars?' he asked them.

'I'm a historian,' said Humphrey. 'I know the scene from a different aspect.'

Tessa looked at him with interest.

'You do like the theatre, though?' she asked. 'Shakespeare, at least?'

'Oh, certainly,' said Humphrey. 'I often come up here.'

The three of them talked about productions they had all seen. Adrian felt left out, and grew bored. He left the room, and the others pulled their stools closer to the table. Tessa poured out more tea, and Patrick cut them each another slice of bread.

'Adrian's edgy,' said Tessa, like the mother of a difficult adolescent. 'It's hard, when you're beginning. You have to get quite tough if you're to succeed.'

'What about the others? You've two more lodgers, haven't you?' Patrick asked.

'Yes. Two men. They're a pair,' said Tessa.

'He's lonely, I suppose,' said Humphrey, nodding towards the door through which Adrian had departed. 'Hasn't he got any friends?'

'It's early in the season. He'll make some,' Tessa said. 'Actually, one of the others I've got here was his friend at first. We've got a triangle.'

'Oh, how inconvenient,' Patrick said.

'Quite.'

'This landlady business is going to be more difficult than you expected, then.'

'Yes. But I'll get the hang of it. I don't take any notice of their moods.'

'It's easier for you, if they're like that,' said Humphrey, looking at her thoughtfully. 'Interested in each other, and not pursuing you.'

'Depends how you look at it,' said Tessa, laughing. 'I like them all, in their different ways.'

She certainly seemed happy enough, despite the problems of her household.

Patrick was wondering how to work round to the subject of the paintings when Humphrey did it for him.

'Patrick told me you had some rather bad paintings which you sold. Have you any more like that? I've got a friend who's interested in dark moorland scenes.'

As he told Patrick later, it was perfectly true, for Patrick was interested.

'No. I got rid of them all. They were terrible,' she said, and appealed to Patrick, 'weren't they?'

'Pretty awful,' he agreed. 'You were lucky anyone took them.'

'Yes. If that man from Stratford hadn't called I'd probably have shoved them all back in the press.'

'What press?'

'That big old press upstairs — we looked at it when you came before, don't you remember?'

'In the press?' Patrick frowned. 'Back in it?'

'Yes. The removal men must have put them in it out of the way. I took them out as I'd decided to use it for linen — sheets and things. I've masses. Tina had enough to stock a hotel. I was going to put them down in the cellar — the paintings, I mean. But it's rather damp — the river, you know.'

'Where did they hang in your aunt's house?' asked Patrick.

'I don't remember seeing them there,' said Tessa. Then she saw what he was getting at. 'You mean maybe they weren't Tina's? Maybe they were here already?' She began to laugh. 'I shouldn't think they were Joss Ruxton's style, either. Maybe they're passed down from owner to owner, like the press. In that case I was jolly lucky to get rid of them so handsomely.' She was completely unperturbed. 'By the way, I found some photographs you might be interested in — they rather confirm Tina's involvement with the theatre. I'll get them.'

She left the room, and they heard her open a drawer in the bureau in the sitting-room. She came back with a faded Kodak folder and drew from it several snapshots. They showed a man and a woman in a narrow street with high buildings in the background.

'It's Venice,' said Humphrey at once.

And the actor with Tina wasn't Sam Irwin: it was Joss Ruxton.

PART 18

I

‘What were you doing in Tessa’s bedroom?’ demanded Humphrey when they drove away.

‘Ha!’ Patrick was delighted at the inference. ‘All perfectly innocent, I assure you. She’d just moved in, and I carried a heavy suitcase upstairs for her. There was this enormous old cupboard in one of the bedrooms.’

‘Tessa’s bedroom.’

‘I don’t know whose it was,’ said Patrick. ‘I just had a look round — you know how curious I am.’

‘I do,’ said Humphrey, far from satisfied.

‘She is rather a nice girl,’ Patrick said.

‘Yes. Nothing special to you, is she?’ Humphrey asked, not that it made any difference.

‘No — not at all. Not my type,’ said Patrick promptly.

But what was his type? That was one of his problems.

‘It’s so difficult,’ Humphrey sighed. ‘One meets these alarming brilliant girls — all so young—’ He did not finish. He was referring to their female pupils. ‘How old would you say she is? Tessa, I mean?’

‘Oh — twenty-six — maybe more. A capable girl.’ Patrick thought of the homely tea.

'And not stupid. Yet not too clever,' Humphrey said. Then he lost heart. 'Still — that happens — you meet a girl like that just once. Never again.'

'I've met her several times,' said Patrick. 'Three, in fact.'

'But I lack your panache in these matters,' said Humphrey. 'I don't know how to proceed.'

'You mean you want to see her again?' Patrick, negotiating a narrow lane, could not spare an eye to glance at his companion. 'Do so, then. Drop in, as we've just done. Or ask her out.'

'But it might be a mistake. I might find I was wrong about her,' said Humphrey, who in the past had often failed to put things to the test.

'Well — no harm done. At least you'd have discovered.'

'She might expect — I don't know.' Humphrey fidgeted with the buckle on his seat-belt.

'You could take her out to dinner. She'd expect no more than a good free meal,' said Patrick stoutly.

'She might refuse to come.'

'She might. If so, you could go and see her and try again, said Patrick.

'She never asked why we'd come today.'

'No. I expect she's quite used to people wanting to see her.'

They drove on in silence for a while, and then Patrick spoke again.

'Jane's quite right, you know,' he said. 'My sister. She say's we're too sheltered — too much protected from life's buffetings. We retreat into the safety of our towers.' And there, battened down, they fed their egos with scholastic triumphs and finicky feuds with their colleagues.

'Women and so forth interfere with one's work,' said Humphrey austerely. 'And one hasn't a pushful nature. One wouldn't have chosen a scholar's life if one was aggressive.'

'Perhaps one wouldn't.'

At what point had he decided on a scholar's life, himself, Patrick wondered. It was really because he had the opportunity, and nothing more attractive beckoned.

'She probably thought us awful fools, acting that scene from the play,' said Humphrey.

'Not at all. She's used to real actors declaiming all over the place. She liked us both,' said Patrick firmly.

'She felt safe with us, just as she does with that young actor. We must seem antique to her,' said Humphrey.

'Speak for yourself,' said Patrick.

'At least you've kept your hair.'

'That's true.' Smugly, Patrick ran a hand over his dark hair, which was still very thick and showed no thread of grey. 'But you're not really bald, Humphrey. You've a receding hairline. And it needn't be a handicap. Plenty of women go for bald men. Think of Kojak.'

Humphrey did, and was not consoled.

Patrick had grown tired of this lonely-hearts talk, and changed the subject.

'You did well over the pictures,' he said. 'I wonder what the police will do now. If they investigate the gallery, they'll have to pick up Gulliver. They'll be lucky if they find any real evidence — or the master-mind behind it all.'

'What are we going to do about it ourselves?' Humphrey asked.

'We're going to look up another young friend of mine — male this time — and make some more enquiries. You aren't in a hurry to get back to Oxford, are you?'

'No — not at all. I'm enjoying myself,' said Humphrey.

'You should get out and about more often,' said Patrick kindly.

By the time they reached Stratford, the office staff had left the theatre and the audience for the evening performance was starting to arrive. Patrick stopped at a telephone box and looked up Denis Vernon's address in the directory. Soon they were ringing the bell of his flat. As they waited for it to be opened, Humphrey said:

'I don't know how you do it. All this dropping in on people, uninvited. I couldn't. They'd be fed up at finding me on the doorstep.'

'Not at all. Why should they be? You're perfectly civilized,' said Patrick.

'I envy you your confidence,' said Humphrey.

'I have an aim, you know. I'm not dropping in without a reason. I'm pursuing information,' Patrick said, and then, 'Ah, Denis,' as the door was opened.

Denis Vernon stood revealed, wearing only a pair of bright orange slacks. Sparse matching hairs adorned his naked chest. He looked surprised to see them.

'Oh — Patrick — come in. I wasn't expecting you,' he said, with some emphasis upon the last word.

Humphrey shot Patrick an 'I told you so' look, but Patrick was undismayed.

'Sorry if we're barging in. I want to ask you something,' he said, stepping across the threshold. 'You remember Humphrey Wilberforce, of course.'

'Yes — hullo,' said Denis, accepting the inevitable and opening the door widely to admit them.

Humphrey was racking his brains to dredge up some memory of the young man. Patrick's description of him had rung no bell, and nor did the actual person. This often happened, he had found; luckily quite a lot of undergraduates he had known were totally forgettable.

'I am expecting someone — we're going to a party,' Denis said. 'Still — never mind. What can I do for you? I was having a shower when you rang.'

'Finish your ablutions, Denis. We can wait,' said Patrick.

'Oh — all right. Find a seat.'

Denis waved them onwards, vanishing himself, and they sank gingerly down on steel-framed chairs with hessian seats which looked fragile, but, once tested, proved comfortable. The flat was very small; the outer door opened into an L-shaped living-room on whose walls hung several surrealist oil paintings of geometric design. There was a stereo record-player and a tape-recorder, and there were two low bookshelves filled mostly with paperbacks.

Humphrey sat back and relaxed. Patrick soon rose and inspected the bookshelves. Then he looked at the paintings and tapped one.

'Not another dummy, surely?' Humphrey said.

'I think not,' said Patrick.

Humming under his breath, he paced about, musing. Humphrey's remarks in the car had surprised him; his social life, or lack of it, was something that Patrick had never thought about. They were colleagues, undemanding friends in the way of men who share a common interest and very often, too, a viewpoint. Each would have described the other as a sound man, one whose support might be sought on some project favoured by the other because they were likely to agree. Now, Humphrey had disclosed a genuine diffidence and Patrick felt vague concern. He must not forget what he had learned.

Denis reappeared wearing a flowered shirt, a pendant round his neck, and smelling of *Brut*.

'There, that's better,' he said. 'Now I'm ready, when she shows up.'

'We won't keep you long, Denis,' said Patrick.

'Can I give you a beer?' Denis asked.

'Yes, please,' said Patrick. If he could spin their stay out, Denis's girl friend might arrive; she could be an actress who would know either Sam, or Joss Ruxton, even both of them. 'She's coming here, is she? Your — er — whoever you're going to this party with? You're not picking her up?'

'She lives miles out in the country. Someone's bringing her in, and I'll take her back.' He grinned in anticipation. 'Roll on midnight,' he said, and went off to the kitchen, which was a narrow slit alongside the bathroom, reappearing promptly with their drinks.

'I wondered what you know about Joss Ruxton,' Patrick asked him, accepting his beer.

'In what way? He's a fine actor and a nice bloke,' said Denis.

'Why isn't he doing Othello this year?'

'No time — still at the Fantasy and he's got a big screen contract. He's filming all day.'

'As simple as that? Didn't he want to repeat last year's success?'

'He'd had enough of it, I think. It's pretty demanding, you know. And there's a lot of money in this film thing. It will make him known all over the world.'

'I see. You don't happen to have the programmes for last year, do you? I don't mean the cast — I mean the programme of performances.'

'I might have. Why?'

'I just want to know which nights different plays were on,' said Patrick.

Denis shrugged, as if to say life was full of people with the weirdest ideas, but he goodnaturedly went to a drawer beside the bookshelves and looked through some papers in it, eventually producing several of the booklets which he handed to Patrick.

'Here you are. The complete set,' he said.

'Thanks,' Patrick accepted them.

'I'll let you have them back in a day or two,' he said. 'Ever had Joss round here?'

'I have, yes. Once or twice, in fact.'

'Did he remark on your pictures? Show any interest?'

'He did, now that you mention it. Wanted to know where I'd got them.'

'And where did you?'

'The artist's a friend of mine. Lives out beyond Warwick. Why do you want to know?'

Patrick changed tack and used the politician's trick of answering one question by asking another.

'You know a lot about acting, don't you, Denis?'

'A bit, yes. I wanted to act myself,' said Denis. 'But then I got diverted on to this side of the business. It was lucky, actually. I'm doing all right as I am — out front's not too easy.'

'You know a lot about the theatre, though. Tell me, how much can one do with make-up?'

'A great deal. What do you want to know? How to stick on a false nose?'

'In a way, yes. You can change your appearance totally, can't you?'

'God, yes. Think of Olivier.'

They did, in respectful silence, for some seconds.

'False noses, as you said, beards and so on. Wigs and spectacles. But more than that — could one be made up to resemble someone else and get away with it?' Patrick demanded.

'Well — you can do certain things. For instance a wig — that's obvious. Dragging the hair up under it and pinning it on top of your head will tilt your nose and give a slight face-lift to a sagging jaw. Eye colour can be changed by wearing contact lenses. You can add height with built-up shoes. You can pad cheeks and adopt a different posture. Then there's voice and expression.' Suddenly Denis pulled his short, straight hair forward over his forehead, relaxed his jaw, raised his voice a few tones, and adopting a slurred accent, said, 'You can become the village yokel, straight out of the Archers, at a stroke.'

His whole appearance was quite changed by the altered voice and the slackening of what was normally a taut, strong jaw-line. Then he thrust a hand through his hair till it stood upright, turned on an ingenuous grin, pretended to be chewing gum, and immediately looked like every Briton's idea of a typical American youth from a university campus or a baseball team.

'It's not difficult,' he said, smoothing his hair down again with a small comb which he took from his shirt pocket. 'You see what you expect to see,' he added. 'Does that answer your question?'

'Yes,' said Patrick. 'Thank you. I think a brilliant actor has been lost.'

Denis looked gratified.

'I was always a good mimic,' he said. 'But what's all this about?'

'I'll tell you when I know the answer,' said Patrick.

At this point the doorbell rang, and Denis bounded over to admit his visitor. The other two, rising slowly, saw him spread his arms wide to enfold her. Only when she was released did they see that it was Tessa Frayne.

II

From a nearby hotel, Patrick telephoned to tell Detective Chief Inspector Frobisher that the suspect paintings were probably at Pear Tree Cottage before Tessa moved in, while Humphrey enquired if there were a table free for dinner.

'Well, the police are moving,' Patrick said, returning to the lounge. 'By tomorrow Gulliver will be in jail.'

'And Joss Ruxton?'

'Who knows? He'll have to be investigated. Though if he was implicated in the robberies he'd never leave stolen paintings in a house he'd sold.'

They went into the restaurant and postponed further discussion until the important matter of choosing their meal was concluded; then, over Humphrey's *pâté maison* and Patrick's smoked trout, they resumed.

'The burgled householder who owned the Corot was in the audience of the Royal Shakespeare Theatre when the robbery took place,' said Patrick. 'Now the police are checking where other people who've recently been robbed of paintings were on the nights their houses were broken into. If they, by coincidence, were in the theatre here too, there could have been someone working behind the scenes — in the box office, or with access to it — tipping the thieves off about bookings. Or it could be an actor who on those nights was not performing.'

'Denis Vernon was in a position to look at the theatre bookings, wasn't he?' Humphrey said. 'And he has an interest in art.' And an interest in Tessa Frayne, he thought balefully.

'Yes. And he knows the area — would be on the spot to reconnoitre likely houses.'

Over the roast duck Hymettus each of them put forward various theories which the other then tried to knock down. They concluded that if an actor were behind the thefts, Brabantio, Desdemona's father, had the best opportunity of completing the robbery, hiding the pictures and returning in time to take the final curtain calls. The programmes would show which plays were performed on the nights of the robberies, and thus which actors were not fully occupied then.

'I don't suppose Joss Ruxton's involved at all,' said Patrick. 'Someone else must have dumped the paintings at the cottage. Tina, for instance.' Or Denis. Or Sam: there was still the packet of tea and the evidence that someone had camped there to be explained. 'Frobisher may get something out of Gulliver.'

'I'm glad they're taking action, not leaving these people free to plan another robbery,' said Humphrey.

'I know, but it seems a pity to scoop up the small fry and risk losing the big boys.'

'Why did you ask Denis Vernon all those questions about make-up?' Humphrey asked.

'Impressive, wasn't he, changing his own appearance like that without a prop or a stick of grease-paint?'

'Very. Confident young chap, and no wonder,' said Humphrey enviously.

'I was wondering how easy it would be for someone well known to be impersonated successfully,' said Patrick.

'I suppose it would depend a bit on who it was and what they had to do,' said Humphrey. 'Isn't there a woman who's often mistaken for the Queen?'

'There was that chap who stood in for Montgomery during the war, wasn't there?' mused Patrick. 'That worked. He was an actor, the substitute, I seem to remember.'

'You're right, I believe,' said Humphrey. 'But what's all this about?'

'It's a long story,' said Patrick. 'It begins with a body in the Thames.'

Through the rhum baba of Humphrey's choice and Patrick's lemon sorbet, he related the tale.

'So that's how you got on to these crooked art dealers? What an extraordinary story.'

'It is.'

'Sounds so improbable — but there was that business of the woman's address in Putney being false.'

'There could be an innocent explanation for that,' said Patrick. 'She might not want to be involved — but she was prepared at the time to step forward and say it was Sam whom the police had plucked from the river.'

'But what do you think really happened? Do you think this friend of yours was impersonating someone and got killed by mistake?'

'I think it's possible.'

'But whom was he impersonating?' Humphrey plainly thought it a fantastic notion.

'I'm not prepared to say just yet,' said Patrick.

'Could he have been mistaken for one of the art thieves? Was there a robbery the night he was killed?' asked Humphrey. 'Maybe he surprised them? Surely that's much more likely? If you're right in assuming, on the strength of a packet of tea, that he'd been at Pear Tree Cottage, that may be what happened.'

'Why chuck him in the Thames, then, with the Avon at your door?'

'Too near home,' said Humphrey promptly. 'That one's easy. Perhaps he was drowned in the Avon first, fished out, and moved. Would a post-mortem show which river it was that had done for him?'

'It might. There would be certain things in certain stretches of river — pollutants and what-not. If you looked for that sort of proof, you'd find it, I expect. In the liver, for instance,' he added, remembering a talk he had had once with a forensic pathologist. He thought of the sacks in the garage at Pear Tree Cottage, and the threads of sacking under the corpse's fingernails. Could this be part of the answer? The sacks had disappeared; it would have been easy for the murderer to collect them after dark. 'This body wasn't drowned, though,' he went on. 'He died from shock — he had arterio-sclerosis — a traumatic fright would have been enough to stop his heart.'

'What a lot of strange things you know,' said Humphrey, who had now become intrigued by the problem himself.

'I wish I knew how Tina Willoughby fits into all this,' said Patrick. 'She's the peg that holds it all together.'

'You'll find out,' said Humphrey.

'Your faith in me is touching,' said Patrick. 'The police don't seem satisfied about Sam, I'm glad to say. They'll sort it out, I expect.'

Before they went back to Oxford they drove up the road, parked near Shakespeare's Birthplace, and walked past Gulliver's Gallery. The narrow entrance to the alley leading to it was dark and shadowy, out of range of the street lights. Patrick pointed it all out to Humphrey.

'We'd better not loiter here, the police are probably watching the place,' he said.

'It's an unobtrusive approach,' said Humphrey. 'If we were thieves hustling in with our loot, we wouldn't be very conspicuous.'

'No. And if Gulliver was waiting inside, canvas and oils at the ready, the new master could be daubed over the old one pretty smartly. He probably has it prepared in advance, or all roughed up on the canvas like that painting by numbers my nephew does. Gulliver turns out those hideosities of the plays by the dozen.'

'In a way I can't help admiring his daring,' said Humphrey.

'You don't mean to say you condone this reprehensible conduct?' Patrick was shocked.

'No. But it's non-violent, and the results must go to people who appreciate them or it wouldn't be happening at all. You can't sell this sort of stuff on the open market.'

'Pride of possession. That's what it's all about,' said Patrick. 'But I'm surprised at you, Humphrey. You must uphold the rule of law.'

'Oh, I do. I'm just impressed by people who live so adventurously,' said the timid don.

As they drove along the A34 and through Shipston-on-Stour, Patrick wondered aloud whether to ask Joss Ruxton about his acquaintance with Tina, as indicated by the photograph of them both in Venice.

'If he's a crook, he won't tell you anything about it. If he isn't crooked, he'll say, "Mind your own damned business",' said Humphrey. 'The police will find all this out now, surely. I should sit tight and wait.'

This was probably sound advice. And there was Manolakis to be thought of, too. He was to go back to Crete at the end of the week. Patrick mentioned this to Humphrey.

'I don't know how he wants to spend the rest of his visit,' he added. He might have decided to remain in London, spending every spare second with Liz. 'We took him to Woburn — my sister and her husband.'

'I didn't know you went in for touring round stately homes,' said Humphrey.

'I don't. I've been to very few. People take you to their local one if you're staying for the weekend and they can't think what to do with you,' said Patrick. 'So I've seen one or two like that. One should do more.'

'I go to them quite often,' said Humphrey. 'Mainly because of the pictures — and sometimes because of the history of the house. It can be an absorbing pastime, and it's one that can be pursued alone. One develops little ploys and interests in odd ways — you know that. You have your spare-time sleuthing. How did that start?'

'Oh — a woman died. I didn't think it was quite straightforward,' said Patrick. 'Other times, I've just happened to be there.'

'You attract these things, though.'

'You mean I put a jinx on events? I hope not. They've usually happened before I appear — I just seem to drop in later.'

'How eerie. I'm glad it doesn't happen to me — I hope it's not catching, like measles.'

Patrick thought that it might be. Perceptions grew sharper with practice.

'Let me know what happens next,' Humphrey urged when they parted in the quadrangle of St Mark's to go to their separate staircases.

'I will,' Patrick promised.

The theory about Sam's death which he had mentioned to Colin as being so unlikely, and which Humphrey had not seriously considered, was now foremost in his mind. Look for evidence, Colin had advised. Before going to bed, Patrick made telephone calls to several London numbers, and as a result of what he learned from these, he resolved to go up again the following day.

While there, he would get in touch with Liz and Manolakis. Naturally.

PART 19

I

The dark red MGB entered London before eight o'clock the following morning. Patrick found a four-hour meter off the Bayswater Road and shovelled money into it; soon afterwards he walked into a new luxury hotel nearby. He carried a large white envelope addressed in typewriting, and with the words 'By Hand' inscribed in the corner. This he gave to the desk clerk, who glanced at it, said, 'I'll see it's delivered right away, sir,' called a page over and said to him, 'Take this up to suite 538 at once.'

How easy it had been! Patrick had expected to follow the envelope with his eyes into a pigeon-hole behind the desk, and had doubted his ability to make out the room number from such a distance.

'Thank you,' he said, moving off. He did not want the man to remember him, but it was a chance he must take. Lest his ruse be discovered, he had put a charity appeal that had been sent to him inside the envelope.

He walked across the foyer and along the passage towards the men's room. He had never been in this hotel before, but reasoning told him he would find some stairs if he kept going. Sure enough, a flight led out of a corner near the cloakrooms.

He ran up them to the first floor, then walked along the corridor until he came to the lift. It was most unlikely that the clerk or anyone in the foyer had noticed him ascending.

Waiters were carrying breakfast trays into rooms as he strode along. The thing was to look confident; bluff could achieve a great deal.

He summoned the lift, and when it arrived, rode up to the fifth floor, where he emerged into a long, straight corridor carpeted in olive green. Numbers on the nearest doors indicated that 538 would be to his left, and he set off, working out his next move as he walked along. Knocking on the door and announcing his own identity would not guarantee admittance; there were too many unpredictables. He paused, tapping a finger against his teeth, indecisive. The pageboy with the mail had probably come and gone already; if not, that might offer an opportunity, or alternatively, breakfast might arrive. The man he sought was unlikely to descend to eat among the common herd. He went on down the corridor, passing room 538, turned at the end and walked back again. As he did so, the door of room 538 opened, a man came out and walked along the passage in the other direction. Patrick continued on behind him, passing the room a second time. Since it was referred to as a suite, there were probably several rooms in use, linked by communicating doors.

The other man went towards the lift, and Patrick turned down a side corridor branching from the main one. A few seconds later he peered cautiously round the corner; the man had disappeared, presumably into the lift. From the far end of the corridor a waiter now appeared, pushing a trolley. Patrick headed back towards room 538 and arrived outside just behind the waiter, whose trolley bore breakfast for two. He tapped at the door and in response to a call from within opened it. He was obviously expected, for it was not locked. Such a possibility had not occurred to Patrick.

'Ah—' he said, and followed the waiter over the threshold before it could be closed, hoping to be taken for one of the proper occupants.

Again, his trick worked. The waiter, who was Spanish, beamed at him, and Patrick followed him through a narrow hallway into a sitting-room where several bowls of flowers stood about; it was clearly the apartment of someone important.

A man in a silk dressing-gown stood looking out of the window, his back to the room.

'Just leave the trolley, please,' he said, without turning. 'Thank you.'

'Thank you, sir,' said the waiter, nodded to Patrick who grinned at him amiably, and left.

The man at the window turned, and the light was behind him, hiding his face, but Patrick knew at once that his theory was right.

'Good morning, Sam,' he said.

II

Sam Irwin put a hand behind him and steadied himself as Patrick stepped forward.

'I'm very glad indeed to find you're not dead after all,' he said.

Sam was speechless.

'How — how on earth—?' he managed at last, but Patrick interrupted.

'That man who went down the corridor. Is he a watchdog?'

'Yes. He does the messages and shopping — I don't go out much. He's gone downstairs to meet someone from the embassy. We don't want people coming up here.'

'I'm sure you don't,' said Patrick. 'If he gets back, I'll play along. You're not Sam, and I'm an old friend you've successfully deceived with your impersonation. Now, what's this all about? And who was in the river?'

Sam had recovered somewhat.

'I've got the part of a lifetime,' he said. 'Taking the place of a man who's been critically ill. If that had been discovered, everything would have gone wrong. He's on the mend now — the plan's been saved. I won't be needed much longer.'

'You've had your meeting?'

'The first one. Now he's got to be persuaded to defect.' Sam gestured. 'He'd like to — but there are ties at home — wife — small child.' Then he looked intently at Patrick. 'How did you know?'

'Your beard,' said Patrick grimly. 'The corpse grew a red beard. A copper I know confirmed that suspicion for me last night. You don't, I'm certain.'

'You mean his showed?'

'Beards go on growing for a short time after death,' said Patrick. 'Who was he?'

Sam looked worried.

'That's the only bit I'm unhappy about,' he said. 'He was very like me — me with my hair dyed, that is. He was an informer — no one meant him to die, but he was caught making a phone call which could have wrecked everything. He died while he was locked up — no one had decided what to do with him. Heart, I suppose.'

The man had died from shock: that much was certain: convenient, though. Patrick had to hurry on, for time was short.

'The identification was fixed,' he said.

'Yes — Leila Waters. She suggested me for the job,' said Sam. 'She'd seen me made up, looking like him. They've used her before to find people for jobs like this. Patrick, you mustn't say anything — it will all be over soon — then I'll reappear, saying I'd lost my memory.'

He made it sound so simple.

'I'll keep your secret as long as it's necessary,' said Patrick, and added, 'what a pity you didn't tell Tina.'

'Tina? Tina Willoughby? Why?'

'She's dead. You didn't know?'

Sam did not: that was obvious.

'How?'

'Suicide. She'd read about your death.'

'But that doesn't make sense. I meant nothing to Tina.

'But you did know her?'

'Yes — through her drink problem. I had one too, once. But she had a thing with Joss Ruxton. They met last year.'

'But that girl — the one he lived with—'

'Which one? There were a series. Tina was just another.'

Patrick stared. Could this be right? Had Joss really picked Tina at forty after a girl in her twenties? Or was it one-sided?

He heard a sound at the outer door. In a flash he was across the room and through the connecting door into a bedroom. As he closed the door softly behind him he heard Sam say, 'I waited to start breakfast till you came back. Well — everything fixed?'

He did not hear the reply but hurried on, into a further bedroom, and from there, went out into the passage. A few minutes later he was walking away down the street.

There had been no time to ask Sam if he had ever been to Pear Tree Cottage.

III

Patrick just missed Liz. She had left for the office five minutes before he arrived at her flat, said Manolakis, who let him in.

'I'm glad you're still here, Dimitri,' said Patrick, temporarily banishing to the back of his mind questions raised in it about the sleeping arrangements at Bolton Gardens. 'I've found Sam Irwin. I want some advice.'

'But, my friend, I know you have found Sam Irwin. This is not news,' said Manolakis.

'He isn't dead,' Patrick said. 'The woman who identified him — the body from the water, that is — she didn't exist. She gave a false name and address. And the one who officially identified him at the inquest committed perjury. I suppose they're both working for Special Branch. Or think they are. I shall have to get on to the police. Sam mustn't go through with this.'

He had taken care to promise Sam only that his secret would be kept as long as was necessary. That allowed plenty of licence for interpretation.

'Sit down and explain,' said Manolakis.

Patrick realized that he had had no breakfast.

'Any coffee going?' he asked.

'Of course. Come along,' said Manolakis, like a kindly housewife.

'You seem quite at home,' Patrick could not resist remarking.

'I am. I am so glad that Elizabeth is not your lady, Patrick. I would not like to walk on your feet.'

'You mean tread on my toes,' said Patrick.

But he had. The fact that he said this proved what had happened.

Patrick hurried on.

'I've been to see him — he's at a hotel—'

'Eat first, then explain,' advised Manolakis, putting bread in the toaster.

Patrick, between mouthfuls of toast and honey, described his abortive visit to Putney, Leila Waters' remark about the colour of Sam's beard, and his own suspicion, since confirmed by Sergeant Bruce, that the corpse must have been a genuine red-headed man, or the postmortem report would have mentioned the inconsistency. There was body hair, not only the beard.

'If it wasn't Sam who was pulled from the river that night, he might be alive. You'd mentioned, in another context, the question of identity. If a dead body was supposed to be Sam's, he might be posing as someone else. I'd seen photographs of him in make-up. I knew what might be done. We've all seen him in his disguise, Dimitri — you, Liz and me — and he's deceived us all.'

Manolakis listened to this intently, nodding his head as Patrick spoke.

'I don't like it, Dimitri. He thinks he's doubling for a man who's ill, for the good of a cause. But Tina didn't commit suicide because she thought he was dead — he was nothing special to her. That newspaper beside her body was a blind. So why did she die?'

'This other actor,' Manolakis said. 'This Joss. It would be good, perhaps, to talk to him.'

'I quite agree. And very likely Detective Chief Inspector Frobisher has already done it, but not about Sam. About the stolen paintings,' Patrick said. 'And I doubt if he had anything at all to do with them.'

IV

An impassive man faced Patrick across a wide desk.

'The matter is out of our hands,' he said. 'Special Branch is dealing with it.'

Patrick had gone from Bolton Gardens to see Sergeant Bruce, who had listened silently to his tale; then he had declared that he had been taken off the case.

'Well, you'd better get back on to it again,' Patrick said roundly. 'A man has died — not the one we thought it was. Two women have given false evidence. Is this how we work here now? I won't believe it. I think Sam's being tricked.'

'Wait, please,' the sergeant had replied, and had left the office. Shortly afterwards, Patrick had been summoned to the presence of the Detective Chief Superintendent who now faced him.

'It's a highly sensitive operation,' the superintendent said. 'One slip, and it will go wrong.'

'But everyone concerned is here, in this country. Why not move at once? Why delay?'

'Correct timing is important,' said the superintendent. 'We both know that things can go wrong — intending detectors have been persuaded back before, by various means.

You must treat this as a matter of the gravest importance, Dr Grant. Secrecy is essential. It's unfortunate that you should have stumbled on the truth.'

Patrick had stumbled nowhere. He had deduced the answer. But quibbling wasted time.

'That woman's death,' he said. 'What's your explanation for that?'

'Depression, probably, or some other commonplace reason,' said the superintendent. 'I must ask you, Dr Grant, to use the utmost discretion in respect of what has been revealed to you.'

Once again a misuse of words, thought Patrick dourly; matters had only been revealed in the sense that he had had eyes to see.

'Well, I'm thankful to find that Sam isn't dead after all, of course,' he said.

'And now, if you don't mind—' The superintendent half rose. 'Sergeant, will you show Dr Grant the way out?'

Sergeant Bruce had been sitting in silence throughout the interview. Now he got up and opened the door. In silence, he followed Patrick out.

'I don't like it. The whole thing reeks,' said Patrick vehemently, when they were in the passage.

'It's out of our hands,' the sergeant repeated.

Patrick went straight from the police station to Scotland Yard, and demanded to see Colin. He had to wait some time.

'I can't spare long — I'm very busy,' Colin said.

'Special Branch has taken over this business about Sam — he's not dead, he's doing an impersonation,' Patrick said.

Colin tidied some papers on his desk.

'The coppers along the road are dropping it,' Patrick told him.

'They must, now,' said Colin. 'You'd better lay off, too, Patrick. My advice is to go back to Oxford and forget the whole thing.'

Patrick was most reluctant to accept this counsel; however, he left Colin to get on with his work and walked round the corner to Westminster Abbey, where Manolakis was waiting for him.

'Let's go and see Joss Ruxton,' he said. He had discovered the actor's address from the telephone directory, the obvious place to look first.

To get there, Patrick had to use the A to Z guide. He wound his way north of St Pancras until he came to a crescent of old brick houses overlooking an oval of grass planted with plane trees.

Joss Ruxton lived in a tall, terraced house with a yellow front door. Patrick rang the bell, and after a short wait it was opened by a woman in a flowered overall.

'Not more police?' she asked at once, standing aggressively in the doorway.

'My name is Grant. I am a fellow of St Mark's College, Oxford. Would you ask Mr Ruxton if he can spare five minutes, please,' said Patrick.

'Well, I don't know,' said the woman, but she went away, leaving them on the step. Soon she returned, and, exuding disapproval, conducted them to a sitting-room which was furnished with old pieces that blended well together. Everything looked cared-for; the wood gleamed; the paintwork was fresh. They sat on a small sofa, side by side, and waited. There were no bookshelves to draw Patrick; in a house this size there was probably room for a study.

Soon, the actor appeared. He entered with a definite flourish, sweeping the door wide before walking in. He was a stocky man, not very tall, with carefully styled thick, greying hair and pale blue eyes.

Patrick introduced himself and Manolakis.

'I understand the police have already been here,' he began, casting his fly immediately upon the water.

'Yes — some nonsense about stolen pictures — they seem to have been dumped in a house I had near Stratford. Nothing to do with me, naturally. The house had been empty some time — the thieves must have broken in and used it as a hiding-place.'

'You sold the house to a friend of yours, Tina Willoughby,' Patrick said, abandoning subtlety. 'You did know her, didn't you?'

'Yes. Did you?' Joss looked at him sharply.

'No, but I heard about her sudden death,' said Patrick.

'It was a terrible shock,' Joss said at once.

'She wasn't depressed, or anything like that?'

'Not at all. She was looking forward to moving,' said Joss.

'She knew Sam Irwin too, didn't she?' Patrick asked.

'Yes — very well — he helped her. She had a problem,' said Joss.

'So I'd heard,' Patrick said. 'You don't think it could have returned? That she did have some mental disturbance?'

'She must have, I suppose,' said Joss. 'What's your interest in all this?'

'I knew Sam,' said Patrick. 'I wondered if she'd done it because of his death.'

'I see. It's possible, I suppose.'

'Well, thanks for confirming that they were acquainted,' said Patrick. 'I'm glad I found you at home.'

'I should be filming,' said the actor. 'But the police delayed me earlier today, so I rang the studio.' He grimaced. 'I've never done such a thing before. Still — there has to be a first time, they say.'

'You're still playing at the Fantasy?'

'Yes — *Henry VIII*,' said Joss.

'You're Henry, of course?'

'Wolsey,' said Joss.

He did not seem unduly distressed at Tina's death, Patrick thought.

The overalled woman was hovering protectively in the hall, waiting to show them out, which she did with some enthusiasm. Patrick drove straight to the police station where he had had such an abortive interview earlier in the day.

'Keep driving round and round,' he said to Manolakis, handing the car over to him when he found no parking slot. 'I'll come out eventually.'

Eyes sparkling, the Greek slid behind the steering-wheel. What a challenge! The London traffic! He glided forward into it, and hoped he would not lose his way, circling in the area.

Patrick went straight to Sergeant Bruce.

'Ah good, you're here,' he said, striding into the office. 'Do you recognize this woman?'

He took the photograph of Tina and Joss Ruxton together in Venice out of his wallet and showed it to the policeman.

Bruce did. His reaction was unmistakable.

'What's this all about?' he asked.

'She's dead. This woman's dead. Suicide, allegedly, but I'm not satisfied.'

The sergeant adopted a wooden expression and said nothing.

'You do know her. I can see that,' Patrick said. 'When did you meet her?'

'If I tell you that her name is Mrs Amy Foster, does that answer your question?' Bruce said, reluctantly.

'It does,' said Patrick, slipping the photograph back. 'And if I tell you that her name was really Mrs Tina Willoughby and that she lived near Maidenhead and died of an over-dose of sleeping pills very recently, does that explain why I want to know?'

'Yes,' said Bruce, and added, 'forget it, sir. It's not our business now.'

'It's my business,' said Patrick grimly. 'I'm not going to see someone set up as a stool pigeon and stand idly by,' and he walked out.

Manolakis, meanwhile, circling around the neighbouring streets, was reflecting grimly that Patrick was now one of just a handful of people who knew that Sam Irwin was in fact alive: such knowledge could be dangerous.

PART 20

I

The words sprang at Patrick from a newspaper placard as he walked towards Sam's hotel.

THEATRICAL AGENT FOUND DEAD.

It meant nothing at first. He walked on. Manolakis had taken the car back to Bolton Gardens, with instructions to park it carefully near Liz's flat. They were to meet there later. Patrick's immediate plan was to lurk about in the hotel in case Sam left, or had any recognizable visitors. At least he would be on the spot and might have a chance to speak to Sam again.

As he went on he saw more hoardings with the same headline, but the message did not register until he read one that said: STAR'S AGENT KILLED IN FALL. Then he bought a paper.

Leila Waters had been found dead early that morning on the pavement beneath her flat.

Patrick felt a sick shock.

Surely Sam would see this news and wonder what had happened? First the man with red hair; then Tina; now Leila Waters.

People were sacrificed in spy operations.

Was this one, and if it was, were these deaths justified? Deaths, as far as he could judge, all in the interests of winning over a possible defector. Surely such a person need only ask for asylum? Other people did not have to be slaughtered to achieve such a result.

At the hotel, Patrick sat in the lounge reading the newspaper item again; it was thought that Leila had slipped while opening the window, which was rather stiff. Well, she might have done, but she must have been used to her own windows.

Patrick turned the facts over in his mind. Leila had, it seemed, willingly helped in the deception over Sam's supposed death; she had suggested him to impersonate the ailing man, and Sam had said she had done such things before. She could be an agent working for Special Branch: or a double-agent. Which was the right answer?

Patrick went to one of the telephones supplied for the use of guests, and asked to be connected with suite 538.

'The suite is empty, sir,' he was told. 'The party checked out this morning.'

The telephonist would not disclose where Sam, in his assumed identity, had gone, and nor would the porter or the desk clerk. They said they did not know.

Patrick swung out of the hotel and went down the road looking for an ordinary telephone box, for he did not want the hotel to overhear him ringing the police.

Colin, at Scotland Yard, was out, so he rang Sergeant Bruce.

'Do you still say we must leave it to Special Branch?' Patrick demanded. 'Who'll be next?'

'I'm sure Special Branch knows what it's doing,' said Bruce in an official sort of voice.

'Well, I'm not,' said Patrick flatly.

He remembered something a policeman had once told him: any corpse found as Sam's supposed body had been, would have been automatically finger-printed. Its identification could have been proved, if the police had wanted to do it. Had they?

II

Manolakis was not back at Bolton Gardens when Patrick returned there, so he could not get in. He paced the kerb outside, until someone came out of the building and he managed to pass through the front door before it fell to and was locked again. He sat on the stairs outside Liz's door, wondering if the Greek had smashed up the MGB.

It seemed a very long time before Manolakis came bounding up the stairs, carrying a large bunch of spring flowers.

'Ah, you have been waiting, my friend,' he said. 'I am sorry. I have been to buy these for Elizabeth.'

'Oh,' said Patrick sourly.

'Your car is safe,' said Manolakis. 'I made mistakes in the road, once, twice, but it was nothing. It is nearby.'

'Good,' said Patrick.

'You seem sad, my friend,' said Manolakis. 'Perhaps you need food? We eat British bacon and eggs.'

He opened Liz's front door and gestured to Patrick to enter.

Probably the sinking sensation in his stomach was merely due to lack of food, Patrick told himself.

'You like British bacon and eggs?' he asked, as once again the Greek took charge of the *cuisine*.

'Very much, he pleases me,' said Manolakis.

Patrick spared time to marvel at how swiftly Liz had domesticated him; at home, he sat back like a pasha while his wife bustled round.

'We must proceed to think laterally,' he said, as the smell of sizzling bacon filled the air.

'Please?' asked Manolakis.

'We need to turn our thoughts outwards,' said Patrick. 'Propound a counter-argument. Sam took on this job thinking it vital. But is that reasonable? Unless the sick man is dying — and Sam says he isn't, even if he was in a critical state — a bedside meeting could have been arranged. It would have been poignant as a publicity stunt. So either the man really is dying, or he isn't ill at all. Perhaps he's already dead. Or perhaps there's another reason for the impersonation, but either way Sam is being deceived.'

Concentrating mightily on both the frying pan and Patrick's words, Manolakis managed to follow most of this.

'Suppose it's Sam, in his disguise, who defects, or appears to,' said Patrick. 'The other way round — behind the iron curtain.'

'If that happened, the real man would step forward and say "Look, here I am."'

'If he's dead, he couldn't,' said Patrick. 'Suppose Special Branch knows that he's dead — been killed, perhaps, to enable all this to be set up — Sam's impersonation couldn't be proved. If he, in his disguise, goes over to the east the truth will never be known. The whole world will be deceived.'

Manolakis slid their fried eggs expertly on to two plates.

'Tonight is the big concert when the two Russians are playing their music,' he said. 'Liz has much wanted to go. She has tickets.' He arranged bacon rashers artistically round the eggs. 'The Russian Embassy will send people, will they not? As a publicity stint?'

'Stunt,' corrected Patrick absently. 'God — you're right, Dimitri — that's where it will be done. In the full eye of the public.'

Even now, Sam would be being coached for his part in it, unaware that he was cast as victim.

'We eat,' said Manolakis prosaically. 'You must go with Liz to the concert. I remain away.'

'But it's you she wants to take,' said Patrick, masochistically.

Manolakis snapped his fingers.

'I am not so fond of music that I must be there,' he said. 'I have the good idea. I take Liz to a Greek restaurant — we come back here afterwards. You go to the concert, with Colin. If Sam is there, you can name him truly. But be careful, my friend. The others who knew also that it is Sam, they are dead.'

PART 21

I

Colin was unavailable, when Patrick tried to get hold of him on the telephone. Frustrated, he rang Humphrey to find out what was happening about the pictures, and learned that Gulliver had been arrested, with his wife and another man who had been at the gallery when the police called, but it was feared some of the larger fry might get away. Tessa Frayne had not, so far, been involved; Humphrey had boldly telephoned her and had arranged to take her out to dinner. At any minute he would be leaving for their appointment.

'I'm not letting young Vernon have it all his own way,' said Humphrey, with rare belligerence.

Patrick, amazed but approving, wished him well, and then, for want of a better idea, telephoned Sergeant Bruce, who, much against his better judgement, agreed that they should meet when he went off duty.

Manolakis then rang Liz at her office and without any trouble at all persuaded her to let Patrick have the concert tickets. On her instructions, he took them from a drawer in her desk and handed them over. Patrick's feelings were ambivalent as he listened to the one-sided conversation.

'Won't you miss Liz when you go home?' he said nastily.

'Very much,' said Manolakis. 'It has been a nice experience.'

Liz might very likely miss Manolakis too, thought Patrick.

'We are good friends,' said the Greek sunnily.

So now he was in some *taverna* with his good friend, and Patrick was in a pub near Charing Cross drinking beer with Sergeant Bruce.

'You can't believe that all those deaths were accidents,' said Patrick.

'Off the record, no,' said Bruce, who knew he should not be here at all, much less discussing such a confidential matter.

If only Patrick himself had looked more closely at the body when it was dragged from the river at the beginning of all this: if it had not been identified as Sam's, the other deaths might not have followed.

'Tina identified that first body. She must have been waiting there on the South Bank, for it to be found, so it can only have been dumped a short while before. It hadn't been in the water long — the beard growth would have been arrested faster if it had, and it showed no signs of prolonged immersion. It might have been brought down in a boat from higher up the river, and slipped out when it got dark. It was tied, perhaps, to something, weighted, and towed.' That might account for the rope marks on the wrists. A diver could have freed it — many things were possible.

'Maybe the murderers planned to fake some sort of accident — some other sort — but the victim dying as he did forced their hand.' Patrick continued to think aloud. 'Now — let's look at it from the other side. Someone from behind the iron curtain wants to defect. He has to wait for an opportunity until he is allowed out of the country on legitimate business. Once that happens, it isn't difficult, is it?'

'Theoretically, no,' said Bruce. 'But if anyone suspected his intentions, he might be forcibly prevented — taken home quickly — at least kept under strict surveillance.'

'Suppose he was a waverer?'

'He'd much better go home if he isn't certain,' said Bruce.

'But suppose he was valuable to us? Suppose if he were persuaded, it would be to our advantage? That might account for Special Branch seeming to condone all this. They could have set the whole thing up.'

Bruce said nothing.

'Tina and Leila both knew that Sam wasn't really dead, so both were working for whoever planned the deception. Both of them knew that a man had, in fact died, although it wasn't Sam. What was important enough for both of them to give false evidence? Something being done in the name of freedom? That must have been the explanation Sam was given. If he accepts it, why shouldn't they? That being so, why are they dead now? And what are Sam's chances?'

Bruce stared at his beer.

'I think all three were being used — deceived about what was at stake. Two are already dead,' said Patrick, 'and Sam's in danger. Let's suppose that the would-be defector isn't one at all, but means to take an important man back with him to the other side, as proof that the West isn't so hot after all. A propaganda coup. The real man won't do it, so he's got rid of, one way or another, and Sam is substituted. He'll be hustled out — doped, perhaps — anyway, given no chance to save himself.'

'Special Branch must have thought of all this,' said Bruce.

'Are you sure? Maybe they believe our first theory, that a defection to the West is planned, and think a few folk are expendable for the good of the majority.'

Bruce did not answer.

'Sam's in fearful danger,' Patrick said. 'I can't just stand aside and let it happen.'

'No, you can't,' Bruce said slowly. 'I'm off duty now. I'll come with you to the concert.'

II

Their seats were at the back of the hall. When they got there, in good time before the concert was due to start, it was still half-empty.

Bruce showed keen interest in the surrounding scene, and told Patrick that he had never been to a concert here before, though he appreciated classical music.

Patrick himself found orchestral and vocal music upsetting; listening to either could be a sensual experience which left him full of vague yearnings he preferred not to define, so he seldom put himself at risk in this way. Tonight, however, he would not be thinking about the music, but about Sam Irwin and the peril he might be in. He glanced at the programme while the sergeant watched the audience arrive.

The concert was to begin with Beethoven's *Spring Sonata* for violin and piano; then Ivan Tamaroff was to play a Chopin *Ballade*. After that, Sasha would play Bach's *Partita no 2 in D minor*. There would be some Debussy for solo piano after the interval, and then the main work, César Franck's *Sonata in A major* for violin and piano.

As Patrick handed the programme to Bruce, a little group of men filed in below them and took seats further down, in the front section of the hall.

'Senator Dawson,' said Bruce.

There was the American whom Patrick had seen at Woburn, with his rimless glasses and close-cut hair. Beside him, Patrick recognized the ambassador. The two talked together, moving to their seats. Behind them were more men, five of them, all in dinner jackets, all also with neat hair cuts and two with spectacles. At first Patrick thought they must be security guards attending the Americans, but Bruce said, 'The East German *chargé d'affaires* and some pals.'

The East Germans, smiling as genially as the Americans, made remarks that were obviously amiable, and all seven men started to chat together. Patrick watched intently as they took their seats, the East Germans in the row behind the Americans. He missed the moment when the two musicians appeared, and was only aware of them when wild applause broke out and the audience rose to its feet.

Ivan Tamaroff, white-haired, smiling, gestured to his son to acknowledge the ovation; in turn, the younger man, slender and dark, deferred to his father.

There was a moment or two while the violinist tuned his fiddle; then they began to play. First one instrument took up the rippling theme, then the other, each player fitting the phrases to his partner. It was a sort of surrender, Patrick thought, each talent laid against the other in total unity; an enviable complement in any sphere.

After the piece the audience was nearly frantic with delight. It was some time before they would settle down to let Ivan, alone at the piano, give them Chopin. His hand seemed to be perfectly recovered; there was no sign of any weakness.

After the Bach, applauding with the rest, Patrick, who had been transported in spite of himself and had almost forgotten why he had come, saw that Senator Dawson had left his seat, though the ambassador was still in his. One of the East Germans had gone too. In a moment Patrick was up and hurrying out of the auditorium himself, with Bruce behind him, and as they went two more men left from the East German group. Hastening after them, Patrick saw them crossing the foyer in the direction of the men's room. He and Bruce followed them inside. The senator and the first East German, a stout man of about fifty, stood side by side, apparently ignoring one another; the other two men took positions on either side of the pair. Bruce formed up alongside, but Patrick merely washed his hands, and when the senator came over to the wash-basin, turned to him.

'Splendid occasion, isn't it?' said Patrick, sounding very British.

'Surely,' said the senator, and Patrick wondered how Sam could speak so distinctly with his cheeks padded.

'We met at Stratford, senator,' said Patrick boldly. 'Do you recollect? At the Birthday celebrations.'

Had it been Sam that day, or the real Senator Dawson, fresh from the conference on pollution of the atmosphere, whom Liz and Manolakis had seen in Shakespeare's Birthday procession? It was certainly Sam at Woburn, showing triumph at the success of his deception when he recognized Patrick and Liz among the tourists.

'We certainly did. I remember it,' said Sam firmly, and then, 'pardon me,' as the East Germans started to leave the cloakroom. His eyes, behind the rimless spectacles, shone with excitement. He left close behind the East German group.

Patrick and Bruce followed. At least, now, if there was trouble, Sam knew friends were near.

In the foyer, some of the audience were forming orderly lines to buy tickets for coffee, and other people were clustering round the bar. Patrick watched the bogus senator chatting to the East Germans.

'What a performance,' he said.

'The place is stiff with Special Branch chaps,' said Bruce. 'They're all over the place. Funny lot of music lovers.'

'I'm thankful they're here,' said Patrick, and then wondered what their presence really meant. What could happen here, under everybody's nose? Would there really be trouble at a cultural occasion? Why should the showdown be tonight? Sam was probably just trying his wings again, as he had at Woburn.

He and Bruce filed back into the hall at the end of the interval and took their seats once more. Ivan, alone, came on to play the Debussy.

As the first notes sounded, Patrick looked down at the seats in front. Senator Dawson was not in his place; nor was the stout middle-aged East German. In that instant, as he watched, the remaining East Germans rose as one man and marched out, to the sound of furious 'Ssshs' from the people around them. Patrick was at once on his feet, running up the stairs to the exit at the top of the hall, with Bruce behind him. They rushed through the door, along the passage and out into the night, finding themselves hurrying downstairs out of the building on a level below the main entrance to the hall.

'Sam must know this area like the back of his hand. He's got that fellow out — he's taking him off somewhere — meeting someone, maybe,' Patrick gasped as they ran.

'The bridge,' cried Bruce, and they both turned to the left.

The East Germans, emerging on the higher level, had a start. Two of them stopped, conferred briefly, then turned back towards Waterloo Bridge; the other two hurried on, with Patrick and the sergeant behind them, towards the narrow footbridge that spanned the river beside the railway. They raced up the stairs that led to the bridge some way behind the East Germans; ahead, footsteps resounded. At this hour, before the theatres and concert halls emptied, the bridge was likely to be deserted, Patrick knew.

A sense of dire urgency caught at him; he raced on, ahead of Bruce, towards whatever lay in front: dim figures in the distance, also running. Then two shots rang out, glaringly loud in the night; no more; and after that, suddenly, the sound of a splash from the river.

Patrick ran on, towards the gunman.

PART 22

I

The body lay sprawling in one of the bays that widened the bridge at intervals: just one body, the fattish middle-aged man, with blood pumping from his chest. He was dead when Patrick reached him. There was no sign of Sam, or of his two pursuers, but sounds of chase came from behind and voices shouted to Patrick and Sergeant Bruce, commanding them to stop.

'Special Branch,' said Bruce, and slowed up.

Patrick ran on and down the first flight of stairs he met at the far side of the bridge. The East Germans might have carried on to the further steps; there was no way of telling. Patrick ran past the Player's Theatre, turned down an alley and saw in front of him the stage door of the Fantasy.

He marched in, past the door-keeper, who was not expecting anyone at this quiet moment during the performance, and was up the stairs looking for the dressing-rooms before anyone had time to challenge him.

Joss Ruxton's had his name on the door. He was inside, sitting before the mirror, wearing a tonsured wig, and dressed in the dark singlet, jeans and boots over which he wore Wolsey's cardinal's robes.

He was only a little out of breath. Actors kept fit.

'Where's Sam?' demanded Patrick.

Joss put a touch of greasepaint on his brow with a hand that did not waver.

'In the river,' he said.

'You shot him.'

'No. The others did. I threw him over the bridge.'

Of course. For if Sam had been found right away, the deception would have been unmasked.

'Senator Dawson — the real senator — is now resting after escaping from a maniac who tried to abduct and assassinate him,' said Joss. In the mirror, his eyes met Patrick's. 'But I don't know how you connected me with this,' he said.

'You killed Tina,' said Patrick. 'You're the only person who could have done that — someone she trusted gave her the sleeping pills, perhaps in a nightcap in bed, then made it look like suicide. But I don't think MI 5 or Special Branch or whatever would stoop to such an act. So you're not working with them.'

'No,' Joss agreed. 'I'm not.'

And then Patrick was looking straight at the barrel of a revolver as the actor turned.

'I can't let you go,' Joss said softly. 'You do see that, I'm sure.'

Patrick's heart gave a shocked leap as the gun pointed steadily at him; the very one, perhaps, that had just shot the stout East German on the bridge. It would be a pity to die without knowing the whole story, he thought calmly, and if he played for time there might be some escape from this. The actor had already shown a touch of vanity in wanting to hear how Patrick had connected him with what had happened, so now he asked another question about Joss's involvement.

'How did you know Sam would be on the bridge?'

'It was the plan,' Joss answered. 'Sam thought he was helping Fedor Schmidt to defect. He thought a car was waiting for them on this side of the river.'

Fedor Schmidt: another pawn in the game.

'Sam knew you'd be waiting for him?'

'Not me personally. Just someone who would take Schmidt to safety. He didn't know I was involved.'

'And why are you?'

But as Patrick asked the question, the answer came to him. Schmidt, dead and so unable to defend himself, would be accused of having tried to assassinate the senator, who would thereby have been proved an enemy of communism. Ever after, the real Senator Dawson would be above suspicion. Because of the risk of accident, a substitute, expendable as Schmidt had been, had been used: an elaborate deception to confirm a Red agent in high office.

If Patrick died now, the plan would succeed. He must survive to have Sam's body taken from the river and properly identified.

With the revolver still pointing at his chest, words came into Patrick's mind.

'"It is the cause, my soul,"' he said aloud.

'Yes,' agreed Ruxton.

How had they got him? It must have happened years ago — in youth, perhaps, and he had waited until now for such an opportunity. For this base end he had first used, then killed, Sam, Tina and Leila — without mercy. Two other men had died also — the original red-haired man, and Schmidt, who perhaps had really wanted to defect.

Patrick decided grimly not to let the list of victims grow.

'If you shoot me now, someone will hear,' he said.

The timing for this night's deed was apt: *Henry VIII* allowed the actor playing Wolsey plenty of time to leave the theatre after the Lord Cardinal's fall from grace before he need return for the final curtain. But the text allowed, at some point, noise and tumult as bidden by the directions. Such a din would drown the sound of shots; Joss would know the moment when he might strike.

Patrick had no weapon now but his wits; and through them he was not unarmed. Here was an adversary who could follow verbal feints.

'"Corruption wins not more than honesty",' he began. 'Perhaps you will dispose of me — but I'm a big man. You won't put me in the river very easily.'

The actor was used, certainly, to sword play on the stage. How would he handle this fight, where Patrick had made the first thrust? He must not drop his guard, or he would be done for, stuffed into a prop basket and smuggled out like Falstaff in *The Merry Wives*, to be dumped anywhere.

'"Farewell to the little good you bear me",' he said. 'But beware. Make sure it's not your own long farewell too.'

'"I hang on no prince's favours",' Ruxton said with scorn, showing only an instant's surprise.

'"On the third day comes a frost, a killing frost",' warned Patrick. He took a step forward and the other did not move. 'How could you put your art to such a use?' he said. 'I've heard you speak some of the finest poetry ever written — witnessed you moving audiences profoundly — what for, in the end? To finish here, with yet another killing? For it will end with me. I'll have been missed already, and plenty of people knew my plans.' At this moment there was small comfort in the thought that even Liz might feel a pang at his demise, though Colin — and Manolakis — would, he hoped, try to avenge him.

But he must concentrate on his foe.

'You have done murder most foul,' he said, and his mind raced. If he could strike a chord in Ruxton, would he falter? As Macbeth he had recently met retribution on the stage; might not the reflex still have power? Actors were superstitious, and many were vain; these weaknesses might linger even if papered over with other creeds. Well, now was the time to screw his courage to the sticking-place with a test.

'"Turn, hellhound, turn,"' Patrick declaimed in a loud voice, and rushed on, amending Macduff's original speech. 'I have but words, my sword is in my words; thou bloodier villain than terms can give thee out—'

As he launched into the lines, uttering them fiercely, Ruxton's hand holding the gun wavered and his expression changed for an instant into bewilderment. In that moment, chancing everything, Patrick went for the gun hand, knocking it upwards with his fist, at the same time ducking sideways. Then he aimed at Ruxton's ankles in a rugger tackle.

The fight that followed was like none he had seen in films or on the stage. It contained grunts, and oaths, but it was over very quickly. Ruxton was used to stage fights with light, athletic men who moved with the throws, not heavy rowing men who pitched their whole weight against him. He went down quickly, dropping the gun at once; Patrick seized his arms and twisted them behind his back. Then he thumped his head hard on the floor.

'That's for Sam,' he said, thickly. 'And that's for poor Tina,' and he gave the actor's head another bang. But he did not want to kill him, so he stopped at that and pinned him on the floor, pressing his arms apart and wondering what to do next.

With rolling eyes, Joss Ruxton glared at him, hissing obscenities as he struggled to break free. Patrick thought that if they stayed like this for long enough, eventually someone would come looking for Cardinal Wolsey to take his curtain call; Ruxton would then escape, for Patrick would be thought an intruder. He gave the tonsured head another thump on the floor for luck, and at that point the door opened.

Sergeant Bruce stood there, and with him were two other men who came on into the dressing-room. One had a gun; the other produced a pair of handcuffs. Bruce followed them in and closed the door.

'I'm delighted to see you,' said Patrick, getting up.

II

By the time Special Branch had finished their questioning, there was not much left of the night. Patrick felt as if he had been put through a mincer. Bruce took him back to his own small flat in Notting Hill, where he slept uneasily for a couple of hours on the sergeant's convertible settee. In the morning, when Bruce had to go on duty, Patrick went round to Bolton Gardens, for Manolakis was due to return to Crete that day.

He was eating yet another large helping of bacon and eggs, with Liz hovering fondly over him.

'I shall miss the English breakfast,' said Manolakis. He looked happy enough at the prospect of going home, and Liz, Patrick decided, trying not to peer too curiously at her, seemed calm even though solicitous.

'How was the concert?' she asked.

Patrick had totally forgotten about the music.

'Oh — very good,' he said.

'I wonder if he'll go back? Sasha, I mean. There's his family to think of, if he stays here with his father.'

Patrick was sure that the young man would stay, and that his wife and baby would be allowed to join him. In return, Joss Ruxton would vanish inexplicably; his appearance in Moscow after some lapse of time would cause a stir, but was the obvious solution to the equation, to avoid a diplomatic incident if he was brought to trial.

Joss, he had learned during the night, had in youth trained as a dancer and had spent two years in Russia as a young man; an ankle injury forced him to stop dancing and he took up acting. He spoke fluent Russian; he might take up his career later in the Russian theatre, or, because his mission had failed, he might never be heard of again.

It was probably the best solution, Patrick reflected. It would be difficult to prove that he had killed Tina and Leila; in the long run less harm might come from the whole incident if it were concluded in a low key. But the real Senator Dawson had yet to be written out of the play, and Special Branch were working on that now.

'Pity about that man having a heart attack,' said Liz. 'It was all too emotional for him, I suppose.'

'Heart attack?' said Patrick cautiously.

'Mm — didn't you know? It was on the news and in the paper. Some Russians and East Germans were in the audience — members of a trade delegation over for a conference. One of them felt ill and had to leave the hall. He died before he could be got to hospital,' said Liz. 'I suppose you were too engrossed to notice.'

'There was some shooting, too, near your Festival Hall,' said Manolakis. 'It is in the paper.'

Patrick picked up Liz's *Guardian*. At the foot of an inner page there was a brief report of the incident Liz had just described; beside it, another small paragraph said that police were investigating a shooting incident on Hungerford Bridge the night before.

'Hm,' said Patrick, noting how both items were placed on the page so that their connection could be inferred.

'Did you solve the identity problem?' Manolakis asked.

'Yes,' said Patrick. 'I'm grateful, Dimitri. You put me on to it. I thought how easy it would be to impersonate Ivan

— with that very distinctive white hair. And he'd had his arm in a sling, to account for not playing. Then Sam was very knowledgeable about music — he could probably talk about it very intelligently.'

'Why was it necessary?' Liz asked.

'If the real Ivan were dead, even ill, Sasha might not have been allowed to leave Russia,' said Patrick.

'But he isn't dead — he played last night. That wasn't Sam.'

'Yes, he did,' said Patrick. 'But remember that bad arm — some sort of infection, wasn't it? Blood poisoning can be serious.'

'So it was Sam whom we saw at Stratford,' said Liz.

'We saw Sam,' Patrick said.

He had not lied to Liz. They had all seen Sam at Woburn. She had made assumptions which he had not contradicted; that was all. For Sam to succeed in the biggest part he had ever played, his secret must be kept to the end, and the last act involving the real senator had not been played.

Manolakis was watching Patrick. There was a glint in his eye. He knows, thought Patrick; he's known all the time.

'You mustn't miss your plane, Dimitri,' he said. 'Are you coming too, Liz?'

'No,' said Liz. 'I'm not. I hate goodbyes.'

III

'You will come to Crete again soon,' said Manolakis, when he had checked in his luggage and stood poised for departure outside the doors that marked the point of no return for travellers.

'Oh yes,' said Patrick.

'And Liz. You will bring her.'

How could Manolakis even suggest such a thing, with his wife and his children impossible to ignore in their own setting? What would Liz feel? But then, he was leaping to conclusions based solely on circumstantial evidence, Patrick reminded himself.

'I don't know her plans,' he said stiffly.

'You are a pair of — what do you call it — silly duffers,' said Manolakis affectionately. 'You are quite suited to each other, you know. But life is pleasant for you, is it not — in your college, with your friends for good talk and your beautiful surroundings.'

He was right. It was safe at Mark's. One knew what to expect, within those ancient walls.

'I'll come, one day,' Patrick promised.

When the Greek had gone, he walked back through the busy terminal building to his car. The first editions of the evening papers were on sale, and he bought one. There might be a fuller report of the previous night's incidents, which must only just have caught the morning papers.

There was no mention of the death of the stout man from his alleged heart attack, nor of the shooting; a paragraph, however, mentioned that Senator Dawson, prominent in the fight against pollution of the atmosphere, had been taken ill in the night and whisked to a private clinic for an emergency operation, the nature of which was not disclosed. His condition was critical.

Ten minutes later, instead of returning to Oxford, Patrick was driving back to London. He found out the name of the clinic by ringing up the paper, and was soon inside its polished, disinfected premises.

Senator Dawson had come round from the operation but was gravely ill; he was allowed no visitors.

While Patrick was being told this, he became aware of a burly man sitting nearby and watching him. It was one of the two who had come with Sergeant Bruce to Ruxton's dressing-room the night before.

Patrick looked him in the eye.

'I am an old friend of the senator's,' he said, turning again to the starched lady who was denying him access. 'As his family is not in this country, he might like to see me.'

He turned again, and regarded the burly special branch man with a steady stare. The man rose.

'I will go up and see,' he said. 'Write down your name and I will tell the senator. He may not, however, be well enough to understand.'

He handed Patrick a small notepad and watched while he wrote on it.

A few minutes later Patrick was being shown into a large room on an upper floor. A figure lay on the high bed, a drip connected to his arm. His face was grey; he seemed to be unconscious, but in one hand he held the piece of paper on which Patrick had written his name. A plain clothes man sat in one corner of the room, and a nurse placed a chair for Patrick beside the bed. He sat down.

After a long time the man on the bed opened his eyes.

'I feel like Sydney Carton,' he said, and smiled faintly.

Sam, shot in the neck, had not been killed the night before. He had to disappear, and Joss had heaved his body over Hungerford Bridge — a feat of strength, for although Sam was light, the rails were high. The shock of immersion had brought him briefly round, and he had kept afloat for the few seconds needed before a river patrol, standing by on orders from Special Branch, rescued him.

Special Branch had already picked up the real senator, who was waiting near the Fantasy Theatre to resume his part as the outraged victim of an attempted assassination.

'You'll get better,' Patrick told Sam.

There were saline drips, blood, all the things needed to save life arranged round him.

Sam shook his head.

'My wife's on her way over,' he said. 'Mrs Dawson,' he added, still speaking with a mid-west drawl. What a performance. 'There's only one ending to this scene.'

It was inevitable. By now the real senator would be dead, Mrs Dawson would see his body appropriately laid out; and the key witness would be gone.

Patrick said, 'You're a great man, senator.'

Sam smiled faintly and shook his head.

'My epitaph must speak for me,' he said. '"I wish no other herald, no other speaker of my living actions—"'

He could not finish the quotation. Patrick said it for him.

'"To keep mine honour from corruption."'

Sam had been used and abused in this last endeavour of his life. And not Sam alone: Leila Waters, deceived into thinking that she was acting for her own masters, had set him up. Tina's fatal role had been ordained when her affair with Joss had begun; thereafter she would do anything to please her lover.

But Special Branch had somehow become suspicious. Patrick was not vain enough to think that his persistent interest in Sam had influenced them; much of his time had been spent pursuing stolen pictures which had nothing to do with Sam's masquerade but which had, by a quirk of fate, been dumped for collection at an empty cottage connected with the case. Sam had been at Pear Tree Cottage briefly, Patrick knew now, hiding out while he rehearsed for his last role. There had been a moment when the official investigation into Sam's alleged death had been halted, and when Patrick had been warned off. Special Branch's involvement could have begun then, or even when the first body was buried, not cremated.

'It was worth it,' Sam said suddenly. '"All that is necessary for the triumph of evil is that good men do nothing."'

A historian and an actor, quoting Burke and Shakespeare as he died, understanding that though he had been tricked he could still emerge the victor: what valour, Patrick thought.

'Senator, please, you must rest,' said the nurse, and to Patrick, 'You'll have to leave.'

How would the authorities persuade the hospital staff to keep quiet about Senator Dawson's gunshot wound, Patrick wondered. Perhaps the assassination story would be allowed to leak, later, when those concerned had all been dealt with. He rose to go, but Sam raised a hand.

'Stay a while,' he said, 'and be my witness.'

Then he closed his eyes.

THE END

AUTHOR'S NOTE

I should like to thank the Marquess of Tavistock for his help and advice, and for consenting to appear in these pages. Every other character, and all the events, are imaginary. My thanks are due, also, to Bill Allan for taking me behind the scenes at the Royal Shakespeare Theatre, and to James Fehr for arranging a concert for me and answering questions about facilities at the Queen Elizabeth Hall.

M.Y.

THE JOFFE BOOKS STORY

We began in 2014 when Jasper agreed to publish his mum's much-rejected romance novel and it became a bestseller.

Since then we've grown into the largest independent publisher in the UK. We're extremely proud to publish some of the very best writers in the world, including Joy Ellis, Faith Martin, Caro Ramsay, Helen Forrester, Simon Brett and Robert Goddard. Everyone at Joffe Books loves reading and we never forget that it all begins with the magic of an author telling a story.

We are proud to publish talented first-time authors, as well as established writers whose books we love introducing to a new generation of readers.

We won Trade Publisher of the Year at the Independent Publishing Awards in 2023 and Best Publisher Award in 2024 at the People's Book Prize. We have been shortlisted for Independent Publisher of the Year at the British Book Awards for the last five years, and were shortlisted for the Diversity and Inclusivity Award at the 2022 Independent Publishing Awards. In 2023 we were shortlisted for Publisher of the Year at the RNA Industry Awards, and in 2024 we were shortlisted at the CWA Daggers for the Best Crime and Mystery Publisher.

We built this company with your help, and we love to hear from you, so please email us about absolutely anything bookish at feedback@joffebooks.com.

If you want to receive free books every Friday and hear about all our new releases, join our mailing list here: www.joffebooks.com/freebooks.

And when you tell your friends about us, just remember: it's pronounced Joffe as in coffee or toffee!

Printed in Dunstable, United Kingdom

77140785R00133